Saving

HER GUARD

a royal house of saene spinoff

KIRU TAYE

Kiru Taye

First Published in Great Britain in 2021 by
LOVE AFRICA PRESS
103 Reaver House, 12 East Street, Epsom KT17 1HX
www.loveafricapress.com

ISBN: 978-1-914226-07-6
Also available as ebook

Dedication

To my readers,
Without you there is no Kiru Taye.

THE PROTECTORS SERIES
Healing His Medic by Nana Prah
Unravelling his Mark by Zee Monodee
Saving Her Guard by Kiru Taye

THE PROTECTORS
Saving
HER GUARD
a royal house of saene spinoff
KIRU TAYE

Blurb

Upstanding royal bodyguard Kojo's primary job is to protect the prime princess of Bagumi from danger. So, when his charge vanishes from her star-studded party at a Lagos hotel, he knows his life won't be worth living if he doesn't find her in one piece. Unfortunately, with inept local law enforcement and dead-end leads, time is running out fast.

Until a chance encounter with a mysterious woman sets his instincts on alert and his heart into overdrive. He's sure the seductive and lethal Latifah holds the answers to his quest. But, how low is he ready to fall to rescue the princess and redeem himself?

This is a Royal House of Saene spinoff and should be read after His Captive Princess (Royal House of Saene #3) to avoid spoilers and for maximum enjoyment.

Chapter 1

Kojo Hamadou walked through the ballroom of the luxury Goldcrest Hotel Suites in Lagos. The scent of exotic flowers filled the air. White and red blossoms sat in thin white vases atop brocade covered tables. His shoes thudded on the shiny hard marble floor. Overhead, chandeliers and spotlights glimmered, making everything dazzle and glow.

The party planners had done well with the classy decorations in preparation for the celebrations this evening. Not that he had an eye for such things except where they hindered or enhanced his job.

In this case, the expensive linens flowing to the floor obscured his line of vision, turning the array of tables into potential hideaways for trouble. He moved through the rows of furniture, checking each table to ensure nothing unexpected lurked beneath the coverings—weapon-toting stowaways or explosive devices.

A little extreme for an engagement party. However, the guests included the crème de la crème of Nigerian high society. Not to mention that the celebrant was a high-born princess and the daughter of the ruler of an African nation.

Added to the mix was the current state of Nigeria as a security hot spot, and he wasn't about to take any chances.

Another man worked the space alongside him from the opposite direction, methodically lifting the brocade cloths and peering underneath as he moved towards Kojo.

Discrete temporary cameras for the closed-circuit security monitors had been installed and checked by Cruz Security Solutions, a firm he collaborated with in Nigeria. In addition, the team had a command base already set up in one of the hotel's conference suites, so they had eyes into the ballroom already.

However, none of the camera angles picked up what lay under the white brocades. Hence the need for this final sweep after the party planners finished decorating and before the event started.

Once they were done, security personnel would stand guard until the doors were officially opened for the party. The guests would have their bags and bodies checked and scanned before being given entry. Each cleared invitee would be given a tagged wristband, which would track their whereabouts during the event if someone had to leave the venue and return.

A mild headache made Kojo's temples throb and his jaw tense. It had been a long hectic week— five straight days of being constantly alert except for the five hours he slept each night.

As the primary protection officer for Her Royal Highness, First Princess Isha Saene of the Kingdom of Bagumi, his job included ensuring all arrangements had been made to secure the venue.

The party was in honour of her recent engagement and organised by her Nigerian best friend Princess Amara Onoh, hence the location.

During international trips, guarding the prime princess required extra effort because he didn't have his usual team alongside. HRH liked to travel without a large entourage. Therefore, creating the need to collaborate with outfits like the Cruz team responsible for Princess Amara's safety.

Still, he would be glad when the trip ended, and they returned to their home country in two days.

He had some R&R downtime coming up.

During the last phone conversation with his mother, she'd complained he hadn't visited for a long while.

Although he was entitled to a week off every quarter, excluding the two-days-a-week rest days, he hadn't taken a holiday in about six months.

Princess Isha's calendar had been filled for the same period. And most of the engagements had been abroad. Since he was Primary, he didn't like delegating her international trips' security to anyone else. So, he tended to take his breaks when she was in Bagumi and on lowkey or palace-based duties.

According to HRH's calendar, she had no more international visits after this Nigerian trip for the next month or so. She would be at home on personal time, finalising her upcoming wedding arrangements.

So, he'd booked to take some time off then. The plan was to spend the long Easter weekend with his parents, brothers, and their families—if his middle sibling wasn't on an active mission. Then, the Tuesday after, he would travel with his friends to Cape Verde for a week before returning to the palace to resume his duties.

A smile curled his lips as he imagined what three bachelors with no obligations could get up for a few days abroad.

"Work hard, play hard," Prince Zik, Isha's second brother, liked to say often. The prince lived the motto.

Kojo worked damned hard, ethos drummed into him by a family of patriotic overachievers. But he rarely had the opportunity to party like the prince did.

So, when his friend suggested the upcoming lads' island trip, Kojo signed up for it. He only had one life, and he might as well enjoy it. Everything shouldn't be about work.

"All clear," the Cruz security personnel said when they completed the checks.

"Good," Kojo replied, satisfied nothing lurked inside that shouldn't be here. "Stay here until Kenny sends the replacements to man the doors. I'm going to walk the perimeter before heading upstairs to check on HRH."

"Sure." The man nodded.

Kojo left him on sentry duty and stepped through the open double glass doors leading to the patio and gardens. The sun was low, casting long shadows in the dusk light.

There were teams upstairs now, guarding the suites where the princesses prepared for the event. So, he could afford to be down here while she was in the safety of the hotel suite surrounded by other bodyguards.

However, the minute Princess Isha left the privacy of her room for the party venue, Kojo would be by her side. When all else failed, it was his job to stand between her and any threats. The danger increased exponentially when she was in public spaces.

But while she was indoors, in her private suite, he could undertake other activities to minimise the risks, like checking the immediate surroundings of the ballroom for any potential hazards.

Taking a deep breath of evening breeze scented with hibiscus, he raised his hands and massaged his temples. Although he wasn't a fan of pills, he would have to take painkillers to ward off the looming migraine and stay focused tonight.

He glanced at his wristwatch, a gift from HRH on his last birthday. The iconic expensive water-resistant timepiece had a stainless-steel case, black rubber strap, a personalised dial, a GPS tracker, and an integral touchscreen. The thing even predicted the weather. He loved it.

A smile curled his lips as he registered the analogue and digital displays on the round dial— Time: eight minutes past six o'clock. Steps: 12,654. Weather: 25ºC and clear skies. Next calendar item: 19:00.

He'd been up for over twelve hours, but his workday wasn't done yet. The party would start in less than an hour.

Turning a corner, he pulled his phone out to call the security suite and let them know he was heading upstairs.

A laundry cart barrelled into his midriff, knocking him back. *Oomph.*

"Oh!" the female cleaner gasped behind a mountain of iron-pressed, folded linen.

"Watch where you're going!" he snapped, his irritability rising as he wondered if he would have to change his whole attire before the event. He was already in formal trousers and shoes. Just needed the dress white shirt and tuxedo jacket to complete the outfit for the occasion.

He looked down, checking himself. He wasn't injured, and his clothes were not damaged. There was a scuff on the hip of black trousers. He rubbed, and it came off quickly. No harm done.

"You can go." He waved a hand for the woman to carry on past him.

"I'm sorry," the husky voice sizzled down his spine, made him stop and pay attention when he would've continued walking.

At first glance, she wasn't remarkable. She was tiny. Her head didn't reach his shoulders. Her midi-length blue-checked pinafore with a company logo hugged abundant curves top and bottom. On her feet were white trainers. Her hair was long, blue-black, with a fringe obscuring half of her chocolate-brown face.

She swiped her cheek with the back of her hand, keeping her face averted, full lips downturned.

Had he upset her? He wasn't usually cranky, but the headache made him snappy. His belly knotted with regret for shouting at her, and he sighed. "I'm sorry for shouting."

Considering her height, how could she even see above the pile of clean laundry? That she had the strength to push the heavy, overloaded trolley astounded him.

"No, it's not your fault." She shook her head, making the hair fly in the wind for a moment, mesmerising him. "I should've been careful. But I was upset."

Their gazes collided. The woman had the most intriguing clear amber eyes he'd ever seen. They caught the light from the outdoor lamps and gleamed with curiosity. Just perfection.

He wanted to get lost in them. But her words prodded him, putting him in protective mode. He glanced in the direction she'd come to see if there was someone there. "Are you okay? Did someone do something to you?"

"No." She paused. "It's just my boss being an asshole. It should be my weekend off work. But he insisted that I come to work and threatened to sack me if I didn't."

"Oh, that's definitely an asshole move," he tried making a joke.

He was rewarded with a smile, the most beautiful smile he'd ever seen. And he'd been hanging around stunning princesses and elite personalities for over a decade.

None of them compared to this cleaner lady.

"Thank you. You're sweet." She was well-spoken too. Her tone lacked any regional inflexions, making it difficult to place her accent. She sounded well-educated and over-qualified to be a cleaner.

Then again, unlike the Bagumian economy, which was thriving, Nigeria's was heading in the opposite direction. The country had a high unemployment rate for young people. So, a university graduate could end up as a cleaner to make ends meet.

"You're welcome," he said. "If it makes you feel better, I'm also working this weekend."

Okay. Now he was flirting. But he couldn't help himself. Everything else was suspended for these few minutes. He would like to extend the time with her and get to know her better.

"Oh, I thought you were a guest. Do you work at the hotel? I haven't seen you before." Her gaze swept over his body and left a trail of heat.

Did she like what she saw?

"I'm not hotel staff." He left it at that, not wanting to divulge confidential information. He couldn't forget his job.

"Oh, okay. I better get back to work." She pushed the trolley, a smile curling her lips. "Nice to meet you, Mr Stranger."

He grinned. He liked her. "It's Kojo, by the way."

"Okay. Nice to meet you, Mr Kojo By-The-Way." She winked and carried on down the path towards the service entrance.

He laughed and chased after her. "Hold up. You haven't told me your name."

"Why do you want to know?" She kept walking.

He wanted to know for personal as well as professional reasons. Since she was working around the party venue, he needed to make sure she was security cleared. And he couldn't do that without knowing her name.

The safety of the princess ranked above his personal life.

But he didn't want her to know he was security yet, so he told her the personal reason. "I would like to know, so I know who to ask for when I come to ask you out on a date."

A smile lit her face as she halted. "You'd like to ask me out on a date?"

"Well, yes. I would like to take you out to a meal, the movies. But we're both working this weekend, and I'll be gone by Sunday night."

"I'd like that." Abandoning the trolley, she stepped up to him. "But how about I come up to your room later when I finish? We can order room service and Netflix and chill."

She trailed her hand down his chest until it rested on his tenting trousers and cupped his dick.

Eyes widening, he sucked in a sharp breath. Even through the fabrics, the feel of her touch was a brand—bold, possessive, erotic. He'd felt nothing like it. Not that he had many sexual encounters with women.

Regardless, one thing was apparent. He craved this woman. Wanted to spend time with her in whatever form it entailed—watching movies or getting laid.

Did she really want him, or was she teasing? He wasn't used to women as brazen as her. He'd been propositioned a few times. Wealthy women seemed to think bodyguards were fair game. Or escorts. But he never entertained them. He didn't want to do anything to taint his family or employer's name.

However, this woman didn't know him or his employer. So, if she wanted him, she wanted Kojo, not the bodyguard for her bed notch.

"You sure?" He sucked in a deep breath. She smelled so sweet. So sexy.

"Yes. What's your room number?" She caressed him.

His breath hitched, and his dick thickened.

"4-1-8." The number came out in a low growl as he fought for some control.

He seemed to be turning into putty in her hands. Or rather, turning into stone. He'd never been so turned on.

"I'll be there around midnight," she said in a sultry voice before stepping away. She shoved the trolley through an open doorway.

He missed her touch immediately. "I still don't know your name."

"It's Grace. Grace Bello." She said but didn't look back.

He watched her walk down the corridor as he raised the phone in his hand. Then he turned away and dialled a number. "Dapo, please check this name in the system for me. Grace Bello."

He waited a few seconds for the other man to do his thing on the computer and get back to him.

"Grace Bello, female, 35, works in hotel support services, employed for three years. No criminal records. No alerts on the system. Is there a problem?" Dapo replied.

"No problem. Thanks." Kojo exhaled in relief.

Grace had cleared security, which meant he could look forward to spending the night with her. He couldn't wait.

Chapter 2

Latifah Kamto slowed her steps along the wide service corridor. White fluorescent bulbs lit the worn, charcoal-painted concrete floor and scuffed grey walls. Empty trolleys lined the right side.

She tilted her head and glanced at the man she'd been talking to seconds ago.

Although he hadn't mentioned his full name or identity, she knew many things about him.

He was born Kojo Andre Hamadou, raised in a family of three male children. His father was currently serving in the armed forces, and his mother was a nurse. He lived in Darusa, the capital city of Bagumi Kingdom, where he worked as Head Royal Guard to the First Princess of the kingdom.

The main reason Latifah had an interest in him? She needed him to achieve the objectives of the current mission.

A mission that would see her executed if caught. Or at the very least imprisoned for life.

But she had been on risky missions before. And the cause was more than worthwhile.

Anyway, she'd become good at evading capture from various authorities. So perhaps her luck would hold out this time too. Although, she strived not to depend on luck and made her own.

Hence, the reason she was watching Kojo now.

His back was turned to her, and his phone lifted to his ear. She wasn't close enough to hear his low voice from this distance. Yet it rumbled in her left ear through the black earpiece hidden behind the stresses of long hair.

"Dapo, please check this name in the system for me. Grace Bello."

The tiny audio transmitter she'd planted inside Kojo's front, right, trouser pocket was working fine then.

Of course, she couldn't hear what the person on the other side of the conversation said. The bug could only pick up sounds around Kojo. If she'd planted it on the collar of his shirt, then she would be able to hear two-way phone chatter.

Her heart raced and sweat popped along her hairline.

She had suspected that he would try to verify her identity. Any bodyguard who knew his job would security-clear their potential love interests. Because anyone who had direct access to him would indirectly have access to his client.

After about a minute, the Dapo on the phone must have verified Latifah's fake name because Kojo said, "No problem. Thanks." And puffed out what sounded like a relieved breath.

"Gotcha," she murmured, a smirk curling her lips at a job well done so far.

It had been a challenging operation to plan, considering there were many factors out of their control. But one of her strengths was the ability to improvise and adapt according to the situation.

She shoved the laundry cart in the direction of the linen room where all the sanitised laundry were kept.

The real Grace Bello had given her the floor map and directions so nothing would go wrong.

With her cover, Latifah had to act like the laundry service employee she was impersonating to avoid suspicion.

First, she pulled the burner phone from her pocket and sent a quick coded message: TB. ST.

Translation: *Target bugged. Stay tuned.*

Returning the phone to her pocket, she unloaded the linen from the trolley and stacked them onto the shelves. A glance around showed that bed sheets were on a different side to the towels. So, she kept the same arrangements. She worked slowly, bidding her time until she got an opening to get to her actual work.

The party for the princess would not start for another twenty minutes even if she didn't account for 'African time'. Then the target needed to come downstairs and mingle before Latifah might get direct access to her. She had hours to kill.

But one thing she'd learned in her previous life as a covert agent was patience. She could spend weeks, even months, waiting for the right—the perfect—opportunity to strike.

Her phone pinged, and she pulled it out of her pocket and read the reply. RT.

Translation: *Roger that.*

Satisfied the rest of the team were on standby, Latifah listened to Kojo make his way upstairs. She could hear everything he did—the rustle of fabric with his movement, the beep of the elevator before he exited it. His greetings to people, probably the bodyguards outside the princesses' suites.

There was the click of a door lock.

"Good evening, My Princess," Kojo said

Latifah pictured him bowing as he greeted the royal.

"Oh, Kojo. There you are."

Latifah recognised Princess Isha's cheery voice.

"Now, we're talking," Latifah muttered under her breath as her pulse rate spiked. She'd known it would be a great idea to bug the bodyguard. He was literally the key to unlocking the kingdom or, in this case, opening the princess's gilded cage so she could be stolen.

"What do you think about these shoes?" Princess Isha's said.

"They both look lovely," Kojo replied.

"That's no help at all," Isha said in an amused voice. "The stylist thinks I should wear this one. But I like this one."

"I'm really not the best person to ask," Kojo replied.

"You don't say." Latifah shook her head as she chuckled.

Men. They had no clue. If a woman asked a man's opinion, it was generally to confirm what she already wanted.

"But I think you should go with the shoe you preferred as you're the one wearing them, not the stylist," Kojo continued speaking.

Latifah gasped, and warmth crept across her chest.

Kojo surprised her with that bit of insight. Perhaps the man understood women just a little.

"Thank you, Kojo." The princess sounded satisfied with his response, same as Latifah.

"You're welcome, Your Highness. If you will excuse me, I need to get ready too."

"Of course. Go ahead."

Fabric rustled as Kojo moved. Then Latifah heard a door open and close. His room must be attached to the princess's suite by a connecting door as he didn't go back into the corridor from the sounds of it.

He opened something and closed it. Then poured liquid into a glass. Water? The sound of shrink-wrap popped, the way tablet popped from a foil wrapper. A gulping sound followed. He was drinking the liquid.

She froze, hand on the shelf, unease worming into her belly.

Did he take a pill? Was he feeling unwell?

There was nothing in his dossier about an underlying health condition. He was a healthy, fit male in his 30s. In his prime.

So, whatever he took would be for something temporary, perhaps some physical ache. A headache?

The royal's schedule for the week had been hectic, which meant Kojo's schedule would be twice as busy.

"Poor darling," she whispered, feeling sympathy for him.

He was just an ordinary person doing his job. Of course, she felt some sympathy for him, especially considering the shitstorm she was about to rain down on him.

Darling? Really, Latifah? Admit it. You're attracted to him.

Latifah puffed a sigh at the little voice in her head.

One of the side effects of being a lone wolf and working a lot by herself. She had whole-ass conversations with herself. Some would call that insanity. She would say it kept her sane.

But maybe, she was losing her damn mind if she referred to her target as 'darling'.

Yes, she was attracted to Kojo. Had been pleasantly surprised at the heat of arousal that swarmed her body when she'd seen him face-to-face. The way he'd looked at her had confirmed he felt the same way.

There was nothing sexier than knowing that the person you craved also craved you.

She smiled now, remembering the way he'd chased after her to find out her name.

So yes, she would admit to having a thing for Kojo Hamadou. There was no shame in it. Two consenting adults and all that jazz.

Kojo was an attractive man. Not in a conventional way. He wasn't a pretty boy like some of the princes in the Royal House of Saene. His nose was a touch too broad, too flat and with a pointy tip for his face to ever be considered pretty.

She wasn't into pretty men, anyway.

No, Kojo seemed to be precisely what she liked. He was a big, brawling man with skin the colour of ebony, about two shades darker than her skin tone.

Legs like tree trunks. Body like a brick wall. Observant eyes that watched her as if no one else existed for the few minutes she'd spoken to him. And full lips she wanted to taste.

Shame that wasn't going to happen.

The sound of running water caught her attention. Sounded like a tap pouring into a sink. She'd head the tinkle into the WC, and now he was washing his hands.

A hygienic man. She liked that. Her smile widened.

She'd tailed enough men to know that many of them didn't wash their hands after using the toilet. Disgusting, the lot of them.

Exactly the reason she never shook strangers' or acquaintances' hands when she could help it.

Kojo hadn't extended his hand for a shake earlier. She would have refused, although she'd wanted the contact. But she'd compensated by caressing his body and the hard bulge in his trousers.

Damn, he was loaded.

Desire flared in her gut, making her nipples harden. She really could use a good tumble between the sheets. Or out of it. She didn't really care too much about having sex in bed. Any flat surface would do—wall, table, floor. As long as it involved pleasure and her favourite brand of...

More fabric rustling in her ear distracted her from the lustful thoughts.

Kojo was changing his clothes.

Shit.

Would he remove the trousers with the bug attached? If he did, then she wouldn't be able to track his movements. This meant she wouldn't be able to track the royal either.

The reason she'd planted the device on him was to keep tabs on Princess Isha's whereabouts through Kojo. Wherever Kojo was tonight, the royal would not be far from him.

Latifah had a spare device in case she needed to bug him again. She'd planned for the eventuality when she'd pretended to accidentally bump into him outside the ballroom.

When she'd seen that he was wearing formal black trousers, she'd hoped it would be the same attire he wore for the party, although his shirt had been pink, not the white required for the event.

However, it was more important that he didn't discover the transmitter. If he did, he would become suspicious, and she might not get the opportunity to get close enough to plant a second device on him.

Now, heart racing, she listened as he dressed.

The sounds from the mic didn't change in relation to his body. So, he must still have the trousers on, although he'd changed his shirt. She heard the soft sighs of the buttons slipping into place. A swish indicated he'd shrugged on a jacket, perhaps.

Beeping like fingers on an electronic keypad, then a pop. The hotel safe?

A slid of metal and a click.

Latifah would recognise that sound anywhere.

Kojo was checking his handgun—the chamber and the magazine. Followed by a soft, whispery slid. He'd just holstered the weapon.

Okay. He would be armed. Good to know.

There had been no weapons on him earlier when they'd interacted. She'd patted him down surreptitiously while she'd groped him as a distraction.

The squeak of a door made Latifah look up and straighten.

A young, dark-skinned man in a busboy uniform walked into the linen room.

She recognised him. Bem. They met when she arrived at the hotel, posing as an employee of the laundry service company the hotel used. She'd told Bem she was covering for a staff member who was off sick. The same staff member whose name she'd given Kojo.

Kojo didn't know Latifah or the Grace woman. And as she'd expected, using the 'Grace' name meant she could be security-verified for the upcoming event a lot quicker than giving a random fake name with no hotel service history.

As long as none of the staff mentioned her fake name in Kojo's presence, everything would be fine.

"All these people that do nonsense. Oh…" Bem trailed off when he saw her, eyes going wide. "It's Aisha, right?"

"Yes," Latifah said, not volunteering anything else. The less information she gave, the less likely her cover would be blown. She focused on him instead and asked in a concerned voice. "Is everything okay?"

"Yes. Well, not really. Front desk called. Apparently, there are blood stains on the bed sheets in room 4-0-7. I swear that was changed already today. Now, I have to go and change them again."

The room he mentioned gave her an idea. She'd already surveyed the hotel layout months ago after they'd found out it would be the party venue. But there was no harm in checking out the floor where the princesses and their entourages were booked. Whoever was in room 4-0-7 was probably one of them. Who knew what she would find out?

"I can imagine the hassle," she said sympathetically. "I can help you change the sheets if you like."

If she went walking around the rooms by herself, someone might stop her and ask questions. But if she was with Bem, who had clearance, it should be easier. Plus, he had a master key which she needed.

"Oh. You want to help." He smiled at her.

"Sure. I don't mind." She touched the linen. "What do you need?"

"Great. Thank you." He glanced down at the digital device in his hand. "I need queen size bottom sheet and top sheet. Quilt cover and pillowcases."

He grabbed a small trolley with cleaning equipment already loaded.

She stacked the linen on top and pushed the trolley. "Come on. Let's go."

"Okay." He led the way out, down the corridor and into the service lift.

She held onto the trolley. It provided a cover and meant people didn't really get a proper look at her. All they would see was a cleaner pushing a trolley.

When they entered the lift, Latifah asked Bem about how long he'd been working here. He seemed happy to oblige.

While nodding to his nonstop chatter, she half-listened to the earpiece.

Kojo was now back in Isha's suite. From the buzz of conversations, other people were there, including Princess Amara, Isha's friend. It seemed they were waiting for the ballroom to fill with guests before heading downstairs.

Latifah and Bem exited the lift on the fourth floor. She allowed the tresses of hair and pile of sheets to obstruct her face.

4-0-7 was closer to the lift than 4-1-8, but she could see down the corridor.

Two beefy men with puffed out chests in black suits and white shirts stood at attention outside what she assumed was Princess Isha's suite. They seemed to be having a conversation and glanced in her direction. She didn't stare directly at them, keeping her gaze averted as Bem knocked on the door to 4-0-7. When there was no reply, he slotted his electronic key in the lock and popped the door open.

He took a plastic wedge from the trolley and propped the door so it stayed open.

Latifah went inside and started stripping the bed with Bem, who continued chatting nonstop. She tuned out of his chatter and listened to the earpiece. She needed to know when Kojo and co would be coming out.

All of a sudden, there was a burst of activity and conversation in the hallway. Kojo and the entourage were heading downstairs.

Latifah straightened just as the first group went past the room door.

The bodyguards that had been outside the doors went past first. Then an elegantly glamourous woman in a cream cocktail dress. Princess Amara.

Latifah used the distraction to slip her hand into Bem jacket pocket and withdrew the master key while his attention was focused on the hallway.

Then two more bodyguards followed by Kojo and Princess Isha in a red ballgown.

As they went past, Kojo glanced into room 4-0-7. His gaze collided with Latifah's. He didn't falter or halt.

Her breath caught as his dark eyes widened with recognition.

Then he was gone.

Only a brief sighting, yet excitement sizzled down her spine, and her heart pounded against her chest. Adrenaline surged inside her.

Seeing him again like this could be dangerous. Yet the possibility was a thrilling aphrodisiac in her veins. It was an awful shame she would not get to fuck the man. Such a damned shame.

But she had a job to do and a princess to kidnap.

She glanced at Bem, who still seemed awestruck. "I'm going to leave you to finish off. I still have work to do downstairs. Is that okay?"

She didn't really care if it was okay with him. But she had to make as little wave as possible.

People tended to remember someone who annoyed them. And she didn't want to be remembered. Not by Bem or any member of the hotel staff. Nothing beyond what she projected, at least.

"Ehm. Of course. I will finish here. Thank you." Bem replied.

"Good." Latifah pushed the trolley and hurried towards the service lift.

The real fun and games were about to begin.

Chapter 3

Standing perfectly still was one of the most natural things for Kojo to do.

Like he was doing this very moment, arms at his back to the beige wall of the glittering ballroom of an exclusive hotel in Lagos.

Around him, the place bustled with merriment at the pre-bachelorette party for First Princess Isha Saene, who was his principal assignment.

His eyes scanned the space in perpetual motion to ensure that nothing was out of place, nobody misbehaving.

The ballroom was full of foreign and local high society. Business moguls and movie stars. Afrobeat artists and international athletes. Celebrities and the crème de la crème. Everything glittered. Women in beautiful expensive gowns and diamond-encrusted jewellery. Men in tuxedos and gold watches.

Kojo was also in a suit—a specially tailored black two-piece with enough space in the jacket to conceal the shoulder holster for the handgun and hidden pockets for the tools of his trade.

One of the perks of being the primary protection officer of the First Princess of Bagumi

Kingdom was that he received a clothing allowance as part of his generous benefits package. It translated to having his work clothes—suits mostly—made to be functional and classy by the royal tailors.

So, he generally blended into any crowd where the princess was present because he dressed the part. However, the fact that he was six-foot-five and built like a rugby prop—a position he played for the royal guards' team—meant he stood out in most crowds.

Still, the elite, invitation-only guest list warranted significant security, which was why he was here along with the team from Cruz Security Solutions. The Cruz team oversaw Princess Amara's protection. She was Princess Isha's friend and the host of the event.

Cold air blasted from the air conditioners. The vast, open windows showed the spotlighted green grassy lawn vista, starry cobalt skies, and indigo waves crashing against white sands.

"Kenny, how's it going at your end?" Kojo spoke into the mouthpiece of the thin headset attached to his left ear.

"All quiet on this end," Kenny Cruz's deep voice came through the earpiece. He was the owner of the security firm. Kojo had known him for over nine years since he started working as Princess Isha's bodyguard. The two men collaborated for occasions like this when their two principals were together or away from home.

"Quiet is exactly how I like it," Kojo replied in a light tone.

Although quiet wasn't referring to the sounds of the party. Instead, it was about everyone behaving themselves, at least no more than what people did at parties.

"Kojo," another voice said in his ear. Luke, another bodyguard, and a Cruz employee. "A server is coming your way to refresh the drinks."

A woman in a black shirt and skirt approached, carrying a magnum of champagne. The blue tagged wristband on her left arm showed she was one of the approved servers for the princesses. They couldn't afford to have the drinks tampered with.

Kojo pulled the small electronic notepad from his pocket, waved the camera and barcode reader over her wrist. A low beep and green LED flashed while her photo and name showed on the screen.

"Go ahead," he said.

Nodding, she walked past, curtsied, and spoke to the ladies clustered around the celebrant and poured the light gold liquid into their crystal flutes.

Kojo hadn't tasted any of the champagne, although it had been flowing readily all evening. He never drank while on duty. Even off duty, he wasn't a heavy drinker.

He came from a long line of royal bodyguards and military people. His father had been head of palace security and was now chief of national security. His first brother, Lumo, was a captain in the air force. His middle sibling, Razi, was a covert agent. The only person in his nuclear family who hadn't been in the security services was his mother. She was the director of nursing at Bagumi Teaching Hospital.

But one thing they all had in common was the service to their nation. As the last offspring, Kojo had grown, knowing he would serve the country in some capacity. However, he hadn't been keen about being in the military when he'd been signed up for army cadets as a teenager. He would have rather just played sports, like other teenagers.

As the last child of successful, patriotic parents, he had an easy middle-class life. He'd attended some of the country's best schools, and his family life had been without many problems. He hadn't been about disrupting the status quo, though.

So, he'd eventually signed up for military service, did the mandatory two years and then requested to be reassigned. Luckily having a father who was top gun in the military service meant he had privileges not accorded others. So, he'd been reassigned to the Royal Guards Division and had landed the relatively cushy role as Princess Isha's personal guard. Nine years later, here he was.

He loved his job. Loved his life. Okay, there was risk involved. Putting his life in jeopardy to guard a VIP. Still, the perks outweighed the inconveniences. He travelled the world and met different people. Although he found it amusing that some of the celebrities tried to seduce him.

The phone in his pocket vibrated. He pulled it out and saw the ID.

Nah, this was one aspect of his job that he didn't enjoy, talking to the person on the other end. With a twist to his mouth, he lifted the phone to his ear.

"Kojo speaking," he answered, keeping emotion out of his voice, and hiding his disdain for the caller.

"I want to speak to Isha," Kweku Doona's arrogant tone came through.

Sometimes Kojo wanted to tell the SOB to eff-off. But he swallowed the words like he'd always done.

"Her Royal Highness Princess Isha is currently indisposed. May I pass on a message," Kojo replied in a snooty tone. He could barely tolerate the man. Mr Doona was uncouth, and Kojo never missed an opportunity to take him down a peg or two, respectfully, of course.

The pompous man was unsuitable for the noble-born eldest daughter of King Ibrahim Saene. However, Kojo understood that sometimes traditions and duty to the kingdom surpassed personal taste.

Still, he was protective over his principal, whom he regarded as more than a job.

"Indisposed? Are you fucking kidding me? I'm her fiancé. Give her the phone immediately, or I will make your life miserable."

"Oh, it's you, Mr Doona. You should have said so from the beginning," Kojo's drawled in an unruffled voice. He was glad his smirk didn't translate into the phone. "If you'll hold on."

He put the phone on mute and strode to the bank of chairs where Princess Isha sat chatting with her friends.

He leaned forward, phone in hand. "Excuse me, Princess."

Princess Isha tilted her head and glanced at him. "Yes?"

"You have a call." He passed the phone over to her. "It's Mr Doona."

She smiled as she took the muted gadget. "Excuse me, ladies. I need to find a quiet space to take this call."

"Sure." Her friends waved her on.

The Bagumian royal got up and sashayed across the lobby, stiletto heels clicking against the marble tiles.

"HRH on the move," Kojo spoke into the mike as he cleared a path to the exit, keeping those who wanted to approach her at bay.

"Roger that. We have eyes on you," Kenny spoke in his ear, indicating the cameras and other security personnel on patrol around the venue.

In the courtyard, the princess walked to a quiet corner amongst the trimmed hibiscus hedges.

The tide lapped against the concrete barrier, and the sea breeze fluttered the hem of his jacket.

Kojo stayed by the double patio doors, posture straight and alert, preventing anyone from coming out so HRH could take the call in relative seclusion. He kept his gaze scanning the view, although he picked up part of the conversation—something about her fiancé running late for the party.

She puffed out a breath. "I'll see you soon."

Puffing out another heavy breath, she lowered the phone and stared at the inky waves only a few meters away. She appeared lost in thought for a few seconds before she swivelled and headed in his direction.

She paused a couple of paces away, her curious expression fixed on him like something worried her.

"Kojo, why do I feel as if you don't like my fiancé?" she asked.

Kojo's face puckered in a frown before it smoothed out. "I have no opinions either way about Mr Doona."

He was her chief of security, which brought a level of familiarity. He was always truthful, albeit mindful where her security might be concerned. In return, she allowed him to do his job without restraint.

"I've never known you to be a liar. Why are you doing so now?" her voice was tart.

Kojo grimaced. "I'm sorry, My Princess. But it is not my place to share my opinions with you." Where her fiancé was concerned, especially.

"Perhaps not. But can you tell me why you always call him Mr Doona?"

"Is that not his name?"

"You know exactly what I mean. He is the president's son. You don't seem to have any respect about that."

Kojo stiffened. "Beyond being the president's son, he is nothing else. Just a man."

Not even a good man at that.

Kojo's spine stiffened, and he tried not to ball his hands into fists when he remembered the reports of Kweku's dishonourable actions. But he would not bring them up now. He would not sully the princess's celebration with ugly truths.

Her eyes glimmered as she seemed to bristle. She'd given him permission to speak freely. Nothing he could do if she didn't like what he said.

"Do you have the same contempt for me? Do you see me as nothing more than the king's daughter?"

Far from it.

He softened his tone. "No, My Princess. You are a princess of Bagumi, a highly placed member of our royal family. Beyond that, you are a much-esteemed ambassador and an advocate. I see your dedication and how you work tirelessly to improve things in Bagumi. I am immensely proud of you and honoured to have the position of being your chief bodyguard."

He was fond of the princess, and in the nine years he'd worked with her, he'd come to regard her more as a kid sister than a job. She was one of the best people he knew—intelligent, compassionate, and determined.

"Thank you, Kojo. However, are you saying that Kweku does not care about his people?"

"I cannot speak for the people of Wanai. I only speak as a Bagumian."

"But?" she prodded.

He hid his smile. She was also highly intuitive. He couldn't forget that.

"But, I have heard rumours about things going on in Wanai and in the Ganuri region, especially."

"What kind of rumours?"

"About ethnic cleansing."

"Lies. Just lies. Think about it. If there was ethnic cleansing going on, why isn't it in the news?

Why isn't the African Union or the United Nations stepping in? Tell me."

"It could be because there's been a blockade and blackout. The government blocked Internet access for the region, and journalists have been banned from going there."

"That's just to stop fake news being spread on the Internet." She shifted uncomfortably. "And a journalist got abducted and killed by the Ganuri militants months ago. The government doesn't want to see anyone else dead."

"The rebels say that the government army was responsible for the killing," Kojo interjected.

Couldn't she see there was more going on than her fiancé was telling her?

"And do you believe the rebels?"

"I don't know. But it seems that if the government doesn't want to be accused of maltreating its citizens, it must be seen to be fair. One way of doing so would be to allow journalists, of course with army protection if necessary, to visit the region and record what is going on. If the rebels are terrorising the locals, then it will become obvious."

The Wanaian government needed to show some good faith to the protestors. Otherwise, the international community should intervene before matters escalated into worse scenarios.

"Thank you, Kojo. I appreciate you speaking your mind with me."

"You're welcome, My Princess," he replied as he held the door for her.

"I will re-join my friends shortly, but first, the ladies' room." She went down the hallway and waited at the threshold while he did a security check of the facilities.

The place was empty and clean. Soft music from hidden speakers piped into the perfumed air. A bouquet of white flowers sat in a lilac vase on the shiny black counter.

He came out and spoke. "All clear."

Princess Isha went inside, and the door swung shut.

Kojo stood outside, arms crossed in front of him.

The squeak of rolling wheels made him glance to the left. A cleaner pushed a large linen trolley down the corridor towards him.

His heart skipped a beat, and his senses heightened in recognition.

"Grace," Kojo said in an unexpectedly husky voice and swallowed to clear the lump in his throat. "What are you doing here?"

"Mr Kojo By-The-Way." She looked up, lips curled in a beguiling smile. "I work here, remember?"

He hadn't thought he would see her again until later. But he'd seen her twice already tonight—in the courtyard and upstairs while he'd escorted the princesses to the party. She'd been in one of the rooms on his floor, changing the bed linen.

If he didn't know better, he'd think she was following him. But her ID had checked out, and Grace Bello was entitled to be around the hotel. The only place she wasn't cleared to enter was the ballroom while the party was underway.

"Of course." He tracked her movement as she headed for the door to the ladies. "You can't go in there."

"I was ordered to clean the toilet because of the event. Unfortunately, there are no fresh towels in there. That's why I brought some." She lifted the stack of towels on the trolley. "Anyway, why are you standing outside the female toilets?"

Of course, she didn't know who he was or his job. He hadn't told her earlier. Then he hadn't been officially on duty. Now he was and had to be all about business.

Grace didn't have the blue tagged wristband, which would automatically grant her access to be in the same vicinity as HRH. So, she couldn't go in without further checks.

"I'm part of the security team for the event. I must clear you before you can go in there. Let me see your badge," Kojo said and examined the trolley—cleaning products and more towels in a compartment with a large empty laundry bag.

If she was going into the same space as the princess, then he had to do his job.

"Oh." Her smile disappeared, her lips pressed tight.

She lifted the lanyard around her neck and pulled the white plastic ID card from the breast pocket. Her fingernails were short, clean and without varnish.

His gut knotted that he'd upset her. Perhaps he should have told her earlier that he was a bodyguard. But his job involved discretion, and he needed to focus on that right now.

He read the name on the tag 'Grace Bello', and the picture was a woman with long black hair fringed to her eyes. She looked like the woman standing before him.

Ignoring his accelerated pulse rate invoked by her presence, he stared at her face, urging his brain to focus on the details he needed to verify ID.

Aside from the fringe that covered almost half of her face, her skin was makeup-free. Freckles dotted her cheeks and around her nose.

He pulled his phone out of his pocket. "Look up. I need to take a photo of your face."

Her body stiffened, the first sign that she was ruffled. Interesting.

She raised her gaze and glared at him. "You don't have permission to take my photograph. That's an invasion of privacy."

"That's the only way I'm going to let you go in there," he replied, keeping his tone matter-of-fact.

Since she hadn't undergone the facial recognition scan required to receive the blue tag, taking her photograph was the next best thing.

But, for a moment, he thought she wouldn't obey.

"Fine. Get on with it." The flirty woman from earlier this evening was gone, replaced by a super annoyed one.

He wanted the flirty woman back. Still, the cautious part of him couldn't just let her through regardless of how attracted he was to her.

He raised the phone, clicked the camera a few times.

She stood still, not fidgeting. Surprising, considering most people were intimidated by his size.

"Do you want to search me as well?" Her tone was half-challenge and half-invitation.

She tilted her determined chin. Her luscious lips were full and curved. The gleam in her eyes seemed to dare him to put his hands on her. Her blue-black hair shimmered in the light.

For a few seconds, he was transfixed, unable to look away. His breath caught in his throat.

His brain seemed to be malfunctioning and couldn't process thoughts coherently. The question he wanted to ask disintegrated, and he couldn't remember the words. The blood pulsed hot and hard in his arteries, heading south, making him throb.

Her eyes, brown with specks of amber, were unwavering, observant, and unafraid.

If he believed in witchcraft, he would think she'd used juju on him. Like she could get him to cater to her every whim.

"Are you done?" Her snarky voice cut through the spell.

Kojo blinked, surprised at his response as his cheeks heated. How could he let himself be distracted?

"You can go in," he said through gritted teeth, pushing the door open so she could disappear and he could get his mind back.

Her lips curled slowly upwards in one corner. Was she smirking? Did she know how much she had affected him?

Grace shoved the trolley past him, and the door swung close.

Damn!

He scrubbed a palm over his head.

"What in the juju hell was that?" he muttered as he exhaled.

He who never mixed work with fun was getting distracted by the promise of pleasure. On the job!

"Come again," Kenny said in his ears, sounding amused.

Shit. Kojo must have depressed the button to turn the headphone on.

"It's nothing. Just getting tired, I guess," he replied.

"It's probably time to take a break. I'll send Luke to cover for you."

Kojo sighed. He did need a break. He'd been on his feet for hours. Maybe that was why he'd been distracted by the woman. Why he'd been thinking of tangling in bedsheets with her instead of focusing on the job.

"Okay. Just wait another ten minutes for HRH to return to the party, then I'll swap with Luke."

"Roger that," came the reply as the door to the bathroom swung open and the trolley rattled out, pushed by Grace.

She stepped around the trolley and into his personal space boldly, her gaze locked on him. The demure woman was gone.

Just like that, their dynamic changed. He was suddenly the one on the defensive.

Flabbergasted, he stepped back, body hitting the wall.

"What are you doing?" his voice came out low, almost a whisper.

She'd groped him earlier. Was she going to do it again? His pulse skyrocketed as he caught her scent—jasmine and something else uniquely her.

Damn. He wanted to bury himself inside her and bask in her warmth.

She wasn't deterred. She pressed her body against his and stood on tiptoes, so her mouth was inches from his.

"I look forward to hanging out later. I'm going to make you feel so good, big guy. Would you like that?" Her voice was sultry. Such a temptation.

He wanted to scream, "yes!" but he clamped his mouth shut, which meant he took huge gulps of air, and her scent permeated him.

Before he could think better of it, his fingers were on her nape, gripping it, and he kissed her. She didn't hesitate or struggle. Instead, she opened for him, tongue invading his mouth, which surprised and thrilled him at the same time.

He gripped her tighter, kissing her harder as his body responded.

The sound of approaching footsteps made him stiffen. He released her, arms raised, ready to shove Grace, but she stepped back, giving him space to breathe.

Annoyance rolled through him. What was wrong with him? He'd just kissed someone while he was on duty. Something he'd never done or even thought about doing. This woman was messing with his head.

"By the way, the princess doesn't want anyone coming in for another ten minutes. You know what I mean."

"What? Is she okay?" He shoved the door open and was hit by a horrible stench.

"She has an upset stomach. You don't want her embarrassed now, do you?" Grace said.

"Of course not." He grumbled and closed the door.

Grace pushed the trolley and called out as she went. "I'll see you later."

His cheeks heated. He'd given his room number, and he *was* looking forward to seeing her again, damn it.

Get your head straight, man.

A woman came round the corner, one of the party guests.

"I'm sorry, madam. This toilet is not in use. Please use the one across the lobby," he said.

He hadn't planned on letting anyone in there anyway until Princess Isha was done. But he hadn't thought she would take this long.

He waited another five minutes, knocked, and walked into the toilet.

"Princess, are you okay?" he asked when he heard nothing. The nasty smell seemed to have dissipated.

No answer. A cold finger slithered down his spine.

One of the cubicles was closed. He knocked on the door. "Your Highness, it's me. Kojo."

Still no answer. Dread curled his stomach.

Had she fainted or something?

He shoved the door, and it gave way, slamming against the partition.

No princess.

What?

He glanced around, shoving the doors to the other cubicles. All empty.

There was no other exit. The ventilation shaft was bolted shut. And she couldn't have vanished into thin air.

Which meant she went out the door. The same door he'd been standing outside.

The trolley. The woman—Grace.

Shit!

He bolted out of the toilet, feet pounding the hard floor of the corridor towards the service staff room.

"Have you seen Grace Bello?" he asked every staff he met.

Nobody had seen her.

"Kenny, can you find the cleaner I was talking to a few minutes ago on the CCTV? It's urgent," he said into the mouthpiece with panting breath.

"What's the matter?" Kenny asked.

"Just find her!" he said in a harsh voice, unwilling to voice the problem for fear of making it real.

"She was last seen heading towards the goods loading bay with a trolley of dirty linen.

"Send backup to the loading bay," Kojo said as he rushed outside, running as fast as he could.

The loading bay was empty, so he ran towards the gates.

"Has anyone left the premises in the last five to ten minutes?" he asked the security men.

"Yes. The laundry van just left." One of them said.

"Did you check it? Who was in it?"

"Just a man and a woman."

"Did you check the back?"

"No. It's normally just towels and linen."

Shit. Kojo growled and turned away as he balled his hands instead of choking the idiot.

Kenny jogged up to him, his expression concerned. "What's going?"

Kojo scrubbed both hands over his face, tugged Kenny away from the security men and voiced his greatest fear in a whisper. "Princess Isha is missing."

And he was a dead man walking.

Chapter 4

"You're not serious." Kenny did the slow jerk, moving his left shoulder away.

"I wish I wasn't." Kojo wished he could go back thirty minutes. Even fifteen minutes would be enough time to get his hands on the Grace woman. "Princess Isha went to the ladies. Then a cleaner arrived with a trolley—"

"Grace Bello?" Kenny asked.

"Yes. Dapo said she'd been cleared earlier. So, I took her photo, checked her trolley, and allowed her into the bathroom. When she came out, I got distracted. I didn't recheck her trolley. Another guest wanted to use the toilet, but I had to redirect her. By the time I checked the bathroom and realised the princess wasn't there, the cleaner was gone."

"Damn," Kenny said, face puckering in a frown. "Let's get back inside. We don't want to alarm the guests."

Kojo followed Kenny, his footsteps heavy as they entered the cool hotel lobby and headed to the command centre, a conference room they'd commandeered for the occasion.

Dapo sat in a chair and swivelled when they walked in. "What's going on?"

Dapo was Kenny's younger brother and worked for the firm. But his speciality was gadgets and gizmos. He loved the techy stuff.

Kenny glanced at Kojo.

Kojo closed his eyes. "Go ahead."

He scrubbed his face and paced the breadth of the space while Kenny explained the situation to his brother.

Stacked monitors displayed different angles of the ballroom. The partygoers all looked like they were having fun, unaware that the celebrant was no longer in the building.

Shit.

Kojo tugged his shirt collar, feeling uncomfortable about his stupid mistake.

How much of a fool was he to fall for the woman's seductive charm so easily? To get so distracted that he didn't bother checking her trolley before she walked away.

"I'll see you later." Her words replayed in his mind.

Yeah, right. Like she would come back after committing a treasonous crime, for which Kojo would now be held accountable.

Losing the princess was an offence equivalent to treason, which was punishable by the death penalty. If something worse happened to the princess, he would be dead. Or persona non grata. Either way, his life would be over. No doubt. And his family would pay a heavy penalty too.

He had to find the princess. And the only clue was the Grace Bello woman. If he saw her again, he would discover Princess Isha's location. Definitely. What other clues were there?

"We have to find the princess." Kojo couldn't imagine anything else.

"Of course, we have to. We have our reputations and livelihoods at stake." Kenny had as much to lose even if his life wasn't at stake.

Losing a client under his watch would cost his firm future work. And he might even lose existing portfolios. But if they found Princess Isha, then their livelihoods could be salvaged.

"The Grace Bello person is the only lead we have. I need the address for the laundry service."

"On it." Dapo typed away on the keyboard.

"I'll send the team to the address," Kenny said. "We'll coordinate the search from here and inform local law enforcement."

"No. You can't do that until I've spoken to the family. Shit." This was the bit Kojo dreaded. How could he tell the royal family that the princess was missing? The fallout. The king had a heart attack recently. This could tip him into a relapse.

This had the potential to be so much worse.

"You're right," Kenny said. "Not a good idea to involve law enforcement yet. They could mess up the investigation. And we don't want this in the media."

"Here's the address." Dapo scribbled on a notepad. "The CCTV images of the woman and the man in the van are not very good. They made sure to avoid the cameras. But I'm printing out the best images we have right now."

"I've sent you're the photo I took of the woman." Kojo didn't need a glossy photo to remember the woman. Her face was imprinted on his mind because of his photographic memory and quick recall. Although since he hadn't seen the man, the photos should help in identifying him.

Kenny grabbed the printouts and spread them on the table. "Send these photos to all our guys electronically, so they are on the alert."

"Will do," Dapo said.

Kojo looked at the first photo shot at the loading bay and analysed the suspect.

A man stood beside the laundry service van. A face cap obscured the top half of his face, but his lips and bearded chin were visible. He was tall and broad but not overly muscular, dressed in the branded uniform of the laundry service. He looked in his late thirties or early forties. His hands were covered in black gloves.

Kojo turned his attention to the photo of the woman. She was dressed like he remembered, bangs over her face and long hair draped around her shoulders as she got into the van. She must have done that on purpose to obscure her face more. He glanced at her hands. She was also wearing black gloves.

He replayed the images of her in the corridor in his mind. Had she been wearing gloves? No. Not when she'd arrived. But after she came out of the toilet, she was wearing gloves as she pushed the trolley away. He must have missed it at the time because he'd been distracted.

She'd pressed against him, touched him. All while the princess was unconscious in the trolley.

He needed his head examined for falling for the trick. It would never happen again.

The point was, Grace and her accomplices were professionals, or at least they appeared professional. Instead of brandishing weapons and trying to overrun the place by brute force, they used stealth. They knew to avoid cameras, obscured their faces to avoid recognition, used gloves to avoid leaving fingerprints or DNA. They had even produced fake ID cards and had gone to the effort of looking like the hotel service contractors.

Unless it was indeed the staff from the laundry company, who had abducted the princess.

He grabbed the sheet off the notepad Dapo had scribbled on and glanced at the address. "I'm going to check out the laundry service offices."

"We have a ballroom full of people waiting for the princess. What do we tell them?" Dapo said.

"Shit," Kojo swore out loud, hand clenched around the paper which crumpled. Of course, that was something else to do, and he still hadn't informed the royal family. "I must call her family in Bagumi."

Kenny laid a hand on his shoulder. "I'll handle things over here and speak to Amara. We'll come up with an excuse for the princess's absence. Go check out the laundry company before the trail gets cold. Just keep me updated. Take Luke with you. He knows Lagos very well."

Luke was the chauffeur assigned to Princess Isha for the week. He was also acting as Kojo's temporary secondary. Kojo was the permanent feature. HRH didn't go anywhere without him.

Until today.

A lump formed in Kojo's throat. He'd really let her down this time. He'd fumbled and dropped the ball. Something he had to fix.

"Thank you," Kojo said. Having backup would come in handy in the unfamiliar territory since Lagos was not his home soil or even in his country. "Heads up. Kweku Doona is arriving soon, and he can be an asshole."

"I can handle assholes." Kenny gave a slight grin. "Go."

"Thanks, man. I appreciate this." Kojo headed for the door, somewhat relieved he wouldn't have to deal with the Doona buffoon or Princess Isha's distraught friends when they found out what happened.

Still, dealing with those wouldn't be as heartbreaking as conveying bad news to the Saene family.

Luke stood outside, waiting by the navy SUV the princess had used all week.

Kojo told him the address and got onto the front passenger seat.

As they got on the way, Kojo explored the options for contacting the palace in Bagumi. He couldn't put it off much longer. They needed to hear the news from him, not from someone else.

The king and the two queens were out of the question, even if he had a direct line to them which he didn't. No one contacted the king directly except members of the royal house or top cabinet officials. He was neither of those.

If he wanted to speak to the king, he would have to go through Zawadi, the oldest of the Saene siblings and the crown prince, which made him out of Kojo's league. He didn't contact the first prince beyond formal settings.

Zareb was the youngest prince and a twin. Although he was Kojo's boss since he was head of palace security, he was the least approachable of the princes. Zareb would sack him on the spot and get him arrested if he called the man and reported that he'd lost the princess. This meant Kojo would lose access to the resources he needed to find the princess.

Zediah, the other twin, wasn't in Bagumi and wasn't involved in security matters, so he wouldn't know what to do in this situation anyway.

That left Azikiwe, who was closest to Isha and the easiest prince to contact. Perhaps he wouldn't want Kojo's head on a chopping block quite yet. At least not if Kojo mentioned he was actively searching for their missing sister. Azikiwe also had enough clout with his siblings to forestall any immediate punitive action against Kojo.

As he pulled out his phone, his conscience niggled. Was he a coward by opting for the route of minimal resistance?

Crown Prince Zawadi would be slighted if Kojo bypassed him and went to Prince Azikiwe. He was always adamant about protocols and hierarchies. Kojo could be digging his own grave if he insulted the crown prince atop losing his sister.

Best to just suck up the dressing-down coming his way rather than incur something worse in the future. He pressed the button for the crown prince's direct line.

"Good evening, Your Highness," Kojo greeted when the call connected.

"Kojo, is everything okay?" Prince Zawadi said. He should have known the royal would detect a problem immediately since Kojo didn't usually contact him.

"I have some bad news." There was no need to delay the inevitable.

"Oh. Hold on." There was rustling, and the background humming quietened.

"What's going on? Where's Isha?" Prince Zawadi asked, seemingly sensing what was coming.

"I'm sorry to say this, Your Highness. Princess Isha is missing?"

"Missing? What do you mean missing?"

Kojo narrated the events, skipping on the part about Grace trying to seduce him. "I'm on the way to the laundry company right now."

There was silence on the line before Prince Zawadi spoke again. "Kojo, I'm immensely disappointed that you allowed my sister to be abducted. We entrusted you with her safety. This news is appalling. I can't imagine what it will do to the rest of the family, especially my father."

Kojo swallowed with difficulty. He was disappointed in himself. "I know, Your Highness. I'm sorry that I let you down. But I promise I will find her."

"What if you don't?" Zawadi said in a heavy voice. "Even if you find her, what is the guarantee that she will be intact?"

Dread seeped ice through Kojo's veins. He gripped the phone tight, making it dig into his flesh.

Honestly, he had no assurances to give. Shouldn't have even made the promise. But what else could he do?

"Then my life is forfeit," he said solemnly. He would find the princess or die trying.

More silence on the line before Zawadi sighed. "Have you spoken to Zareb?"

It seemed the prince accepted his vow, even if he wasn't convinced. "Not yet. I wanted to talk to you first."

"Okay. I'll speak to them. Unfortunately, because of the king, we must keep this quiet for now. So, make sure it stays out of the news. It also means you can't use local law enforcement. I'll speak to the BIS so we can use covert resources and liaise with the Nigerian Security Services."

"Can I ask for Razi to be assigned to this case? I'm going to call him, but I would rather he was officially authorised."

His brother Razi worked at the Bagumi Intelligence Service. So, they would be able to cut through bureaucratic issues with their Nigerian counterparts about gathering information. Plus, he needed his brother's expertise in conducting the investigation.

"Of course, you can have whatever resources you need. Just find my sister and bring her home safely."

Prince Zawadi's words were both an order and a threat. Kojo didn't miss that.

"I will. Thank you, Your Highness."

"Keep me updated."

"Yes, Your Highness."

The line went dead.

Kojo sagged into the seat, somewhat relieved he hadn't been ordered to return to Bagumi immediately to answer for his misdeeds. He closed his eyes, but the sounds of Lagos nightlife didn't let him settle, and he opened them again.

They got snagged in traffic, but Luke found an alternative route through back roads, something Kojo wouldn't have known to do. Forty minutes later, they pulled up outside a two-level building on a large plot not far from the main road. Luke stopped next to the perimeter wall.

Kojo got out of the vehicle and surveyed the area. There were shops and other businesses on either side of the road, all closed, considering it was after nine post-meridiem.

Luke joined him by the slightly ajar grey gates.

"Stay alert," Kojo said and pushed the creaking metal barrier.

He didn't know what to expect inside. There was a car in the driveway, but the place looked deserted. Dull orange lit the concrete driveway, although he couldn't see any illuminations through the windows.

He tried the front door, which rattled and stayed locked. He indicated for Luke to take the right side of the building while he went down the left. The narrow passage was dark. So, he pulled his phone out and used the torch.

A door stood to the side of the building. Kojo pushed the panel, and it swung open, revealing a dark, empty corridor.

Pressing the button on his phone, he called Luke.

The man answered immediately. "Yes."

"I found an entry point," Kojo said into the Bluetooth headset.

"I'm coming to you."

Kojo waited. He didn't know what he would find inside the house. The open front gate and side door indicated this might be a trap.

In the nine years he'd been a royal bodyguard, the worst he'd had to deal with was crowd control, ferrying the princess through screaming fans and jubilant citizens. But those people hadn't intended any harm, just wanted the princess's attention.

None of it had been life and death situations. He'd never worried about walking into premises where he could get a bullet in the chest.

He patted his chest, grateful for the force of habit that made him wear a bullet-proof vest daily even when there'd never been any direct danger.

Until now.

Luke came around the corner, phone in hand, torch cutting a path through the dark passage.

"This could be a trap. So be on the lookout," Kojo said.

"Will do."

Kojo pushed the door slowly. It opened into a dark corridor. Phone torch in one hand, he entered, taking slow ginger steps.

"I'll go up," Luke mouthed and headed up the stairs.

Kojo surveyed the ground floor. There was a kitchen, a staff room and changing room—all empty.

The last door led into what looked like a laundry room. There were industrial washing machines stacked against the wall.

He swept his torch in a wide arch, and it beamed on two people bound onto chairs, tapes around their mouths. Muffled noises came from them. Perhaps sobs and pleading.

His heart skipped a beat.

"Over here," he shouted for Luke, scanning the wall for the light switch. He found it and flicked it on, closing one eye to help his dark-to-light vision. White light flooded the place as Luke ran in.

The man and woman blinked, averting their gazes from the glare. They must have been in the dark for long.

Kojo approached cautiously. "I'm here to help. Not going to hurt you. I'm just going to take the tape off your mouth. Okay?"

The man nodded, and Kojo picked a corner of the duct tape and ripped it off.

The man groaned as he worked his jaw muscles.

"My name is Kojo, and I'm from Goldcrest Hotel. Who are you, and what happened here?" he asked, raised his phone and took snapshots of them.

He sent the photos to Kenny to verify if any of the hotel staff knew them.

The man blinked. "My name is Animashaun. This is my business. We were attacked by some people this evening. They tied us up for hours and took our van. One of them was here until very recently. When you came in just now, I thought you were him."

Kojo pulled out his flip knife. The woman's eyes went wide, and she jerked in her chair violently.

"Calm down. I'm just going to cut the tapes off."

They sat still as he sliced off the bindings from their arms and legs.

"What's your name?" he asked the woman when she removed the gag.

"Grace Bello," she replied, rubbing her arms.

Of course, it made sense the abductors would impersonate the real laundry workers. But how come the hotel staff didn't notice that the two Graces didn't match?

He found the picture of the Grace-impersonator he'd taken plus the ones Dapo had sent to his phone and presented them. "Do you recognise these people?"

Grace looked at the photo of the woman. "Yes, she was here. But she left a long time ago."

"What time?"

"Maybe about 5 o'clock."

"What about him?" He showed the other photo.

Grace shook her head. "I've never seen him before."

Kojo frowned. "Are you sure?"

"Yes."

"What about you, Mr Animashaun?" Kojo asked the man whose gaze seemed fixed on a blue-white-red striped plastic bag in the corner.

"Sorry, what?" the man asked, his gaze averted in a guilty expression.

What was the man hiding?

"Have you seen this man?" Kojo asked, lifting the phone so the laundry service owner could see better. He looked at Luke, who stood by the door and nodded towards the bag.

Luke understood and went to examine the bag.

"No," Mr Animashaun said. "He wasn't the man who was here this evening. The man that was here was younger, maybe in his thirties, and he was bigger too. Although most of his face was covered by the scarf and hat, I heard his voice."

"Can you describe him?"

"He was taller than you. Maybe not as big. He wore overalls like a mechanic. It was his voice that stood out for me. I couldn't recognise his accent. He didn't sound Nigerian. He spoke in pidgin English, but it was different from the Lagos pidgin."

Luke brought the bag over.

"Don't touch that," the business owner protested.

"What is it?" Kojo asked, turning towards Luke as he placed the bag on a closed washing machine.

"It's nothing," Animashaun replied.

Luke opened the bag and took out a wad of crisp banknotes. "This isn't nothing. There's probably over a million naira in here."

The man averted his gaze.

Kojo looked inside. The bag was packed with one thousand naira notes in bundles of fifty, and there were about twenty of them.

"Mr Animashaun, this evening some people attempted an armed robbery at Goldcrest Hotel using your company van. The state governor's wife was there. You can imagine the trouble coming." Kojo couldn't vocalise what really happened. Using the First Lady was a diversion, and armed robbery was as close to the truth as he was willing to go. "Did you have something to do with it?"

"No! *Olorun maje!*" the man denied vehemently, shaking his head. "My hands are clean."

"Tell me what this money is doing here, or you will both spend the night in police custody."

"Ah! It's the people that tied us up that brought the bag," Grace said, gesticulating. "Mr Animashaun, tell them, na."

"I will talk," the man said. "The people brought the bag of money. They said it was compensation for taking our van and inconveniencing us. That's all."

"So, you let them use your van as a getaway vehicle, and they used your IDs to get into the hotel. You know you're guilty of conspiracy to commit armed robbery."

"No, we didn't know what they were going to do. And we were tied up. One of them stayed here with a gun. You saw us when you came. We were tied up. If you didn't show up, I don't' know how we would have got out tonight."

Kojo doubted that they were directly involved with the abduction. But frustration lanced him because he was still no nearer to finding the princess.

"So, they have no intention of returning your van. Does it have a tracker installed?" he asked in hope.

"Yes, yes. If I get my phone, I can show you where it is on the map."

"Okay. Do that."

The man left, and Luke followed him.

"Is it okay if I used the ladies," Grace said.

"Sure," Kojo said.

When she left, Kojo grabbed his phone and called Kenny.

Chapter 5

Latifah lived for adventure.

The second daughter to a long-serving military officer, she was everything her sister wasn't.

When they'd been young girls, people had remarked at how different they'd been.

Her sister, Nabou, was studious and had been great academically, while Latifah had found the classroom stifling. She'd yearned for adventure to faraway places and had been bored of school and all the usual things girls were interested in.

Until her parents had made the decision to send her to a military academy where she had excelled. She'd graduated and served as an officer for many years, even gotten decorated. She'd worked as an undercover investigator, infiltrating organised crime syndicates, people trafficking rings and religious fundamentalists groups.

She'd put her life on the line on several occasions to protect the innocent and had the scars as souvenirs.

But she'd started falling out of love with military service when she'd seen the way the army grunts in her country had brutalised civilians. She'd investigated and reported many of them, but nothing had been done to them.

Then the Wanai Secret Police had arrested her cousin Zain Bassong under false charges, detained and tortured him on several occasions for his political views.

That had been the last straw.

In frustration, she'd resigned her commission and joined him to set up the revolutionary group, the Movement for the Liberation of Ganuri. Their goals—to dispose of the current Wanaian president and his family or create a new nation of Ganuri, whichever came first.

So here she was, in Nigeria, having committed several crimes today. Most prominent—the abduction of a high-ranking member of a royal family and shipping the captive across international borders.

Latifah was usually on the other side—serving on the side of the government. On the side of the law.

But life wasn't always black or white, and she mainly lived in the grey area these days.

Anyway, the Wanaian law was an ass. The system was corrupt and polluted, only catering for the people in power while the masses suffered.

Over the past nine years, the MLG had tried to affect change through legal means, the courts, and peaceful protests. None of it worked.

Instead, things had gotten worse, and the government now blatantly killed innocent civilians out on the streets without any recourse.

It was time for something different. A drastic approach. A reckoning.

Hence the need to abduct the First Princess of the Bagumi Kingdom, who was engaged to the Wanaian President's son. She would be a bargaining chip, a tool to persuade the tormentors to desist from their actions.

As a group, they had planned and executed the mission with minimal hitches. Now, the target was in custody and on a flight to Wanai.

Latifah understood the consequence of their actions was death.

But this wasn't about their personal conveniences.

This was about the people of Wanai, a people currently suffering under the brutal rule of a dictator. The president was systematically wiping out the Ganuri tribe through ethnic cleansing and genocide.

The rest of the world was standing by and letting it happen.

So Latifah and other vital members of the MLG had taken it into their hands to do something radical to highlight the problem in the country.

Now, Latifah drove the blacked-out SUV back to the safehouse in Festac Town, a moderately affordable community in Lagos state. She would spend the night and then start her journey back to Wanai tomorrow.

The outdoor security lights came on, indicating that there was an electricity supply. Nigeria tended to have an intermittent service. But the owner of the property had guaranteed that there would be a constant supply of power. Latifah didn't care if it was from the power grid or local generator as long as she could have a comfortable night with the fan or air conditioner.

She'd booked the duplex through an online lodgings marketplace for the whole week. The place was stocked with food and toiletries as well as the furnishings as per her request.

She'd used the service many times before and never had a problem.

Wearing gloves, Latifah pulled the keys from her pocket and opened the security barrier and front door. The entrance led into a living room with cream walls. She headed straight for the bedroom, dumped her overnight bag on the divan and stripped her clothes. The idea was to use as little space as possible and leave as little forensics as possible.

It wasn't the Nigerian authorities she feared. They were more interested in lining the pockets of terrorists and criminals with ransom money to investigate her actions properly.

No, it was the Bagumians that concerned her. Their history proved they were least likely to negotiate or treat her with kid gloves. Instead, they would use all the resources at their disposal to hunt her down once they established her identity. Including using the Interpol network and bringing in foreign experts to follow her trail.

She'd already made an error by letting the bodyguard take a photograph of her face. Though, she'd had prosthetics that altered her features at the time.

Still, it couldn't be helped. It had been the only way to get into the bathroom so she could take the princess and the first real opportunity they'd had all night. Another opening like that would have been impossible.

So, she had to be careful. She would have to wipe down every surface she touched and burn anything else she couldn't clean.

Minutes later, she was washed and wearing loose cotton shorts and a t-shirt. She needed sleep after the last few hectic days. She climbed into bed as her phone beeped.

She picked it from the bedside and checked the alarm reminding her of the time.

Midnight.

Kojo. She'd told him she would meet him now.

Shame she wouldn't be keeping the promise to him. It would've been a fantastic night exploring each other. Instead, she was lying low.

The image of the hunk of a man filled her mind—his hardness, his arresting gaze, his sweetness. All the sexy things she could've done with him.

Damn. Temptation pulsed in her core, making her itch to get in the car and drive back to the hotel just to find out.

Laughter bubbled out of her mouth.

Sure, she was adventurous, but she wasn't crazy.

The mission was more important than getting her kicks, and she would have to find release some other way.

As compensation, she logged into the app and checked the location of the bug she had planted on him. Unfortunately, it had a short-range audio transmission but still showed the location of the target.

Right now, sweet Mr Kojo was at the Goldcrest Hotel Suites, probably in his room. She wished she could hear him moving around like she'd done earlier. If she'd spent the night at the hotel, she would be able to tap into the audio frequency and listen to him from the bug planted in his trouser pocket.

The device had been handy.

Once the princess had headed for the toilets, the tracker had indicated Kojo's location. This had been Latifah's cue to head in their direction. And by using her seduction charms on the man after she'd exited the bathrooms, she'd ensured he didn't search the trolley, which she'd suspected he would do.

Now, he wouldn't be waiting up for her since he had other more urgent matters at hand.

Latifah had upended Kojo's life by snatching the princess. His job would be on the line.

A twinge of guilt assaulted her. She wasn't in the business of causing harm to innocent people. In fact, this mission was about saving the vulnerable citizens of Wanai who were currently under the brutal, despotic government of a dictator.

They'd needed a political ace card, and the princess was it, unfortunately.

However, Latifah would admit abducting Princess Isha would cause distress and discomfort to her family and friends. The reason she'd found a late-night internet café earlier and sent an encoded message to the Saene royal family letting them know Princess Isha was safe.

Hopefully, that would ease their minds until the princess returned home.

Still, the thought didn't ease Latifah's mind. Perturbed, she tossed and turned until sleep finally claimed her.

***

Latifah woke with the image of the giant man filling her vision, sweat trickling between her breasts, making her clothes cling to damp flesh.

Kojo was all solidity and strength, making her mouth water and her insides clench as she hovered between dream and memories.

A smile curled her lips, and her clit throbbed at the feel of his body and the brief, passionate kiss they'd shared in the hotel corridor outside the ladies'.

Her heart had pounded so fast, and she'd been intoxicated with arousal at the danger of discovery. It had been a double-edged sword—wanting to screw Kojo against the wall. Yet, needing to get away as quickly as possible with the illicit bundle covered with towels in the laundry cart.

Warmth pulsed through her when she remembered the taste of his lips. How would his mouth feel on the rest of her body—breasts, stomach, and pussy?

"Oh," she moaned, sliding a hand into her shorts, and finding slick flesh. Her thighs fell apart as she parted her labia. Fingers circled the sensitive nerve-filled button at her centre before dipping into her slit.

Excitement raced through her as she pictured Kojo. His swagger as he'd walked past room 4-0-7. His sexy, crinkled smile when she'd first met him. His broad shoulders and thick arms as he'd held her against his body.

She'd observed every detail of his tailored suit stretched across his body as he'd scrutinised her ID. The tightness of his trousers against his butt and thighs. The feel of his hardened erection through the fabric of his pants.

She bit her bottom lip as the memories played back, pumping fingers into her wet pussy while circling and teasing her clit with her thumb. Clenching tightly around her digits, her hips canting in rhythm.

She imagined Kojo's dark observant eyes staring straight at her, watching her as she pleasured herself, his dick swollen and needy of her body. He would fight for control, not wanting to succumb to her. Yet, his body would betray him. His shaft would swell with the desire to seek completion. His mouth would water with wanting to taste her.

With the image of his eyes burning into her, she thrust faster, clenched tighter as the orgasm crashed over her and a long moan burst from her lips.

Closing her eyes, she took calming breaths to calm her racing heart as she withdrew her hand and drifted back to sleep.

***

The following morning Latifah got up and took out the cleaning items. First, she vacuum-cleaned the interior of the house and the car. Then she scrubbed every surface, wiping out any lingering DNA or fingerprints she or her colleagues may have left behind.

Afterwards, she booked a taxi, showered, dressed, and packed everything into the overnight bag. Then she burned the bedsheets and linen she'd used.

When the cab driver messaged he was outside, she wiped the surfaces to remove her fingerprints, locked the door and headed towards the gates.

There was plenty of time to catch her flight to Accra and then cross the border into Wanai by road.

She stepped through the gates, walked towards the Toyota Corolla parked outside the building. Instinct made her glance to the side. Her heart froze in shock at the sight of the man standing beside the entrance.

Adrenaline propelled her forward across the pavement. She jumped into the backseat of the car and shouted at the driver to go.

But it was too late.

Chapter 6

The morning after Princess Isha went missing, Kojo was back in the SUV with Luke.

Last night had been a hive of activities.

Thanks to the tracker on the laundry service van. Dapo had been able to approximate the last known location of the vehicle. Unfortunately, they'd found it burnt out and abandoned by a quiet country lane, making it impossible to recover any fingerprints or DNA.

On a positive note, they'd recovered the bag of money given to Mr Animashaun, and Kenny's team were dealing with the lab analysis.

Kojo had returned to the hotel and dealt with Kweku Doona, who proved to be a hindrance rather than a help, with his bluster. A good thing they were not in Wanai as the annoying man would have been able to take over the investigation.

Later, in the quiet of his room, Kojo had called his brother and left a message on his answering service. Razi was an undercover agent. When he was on a mission, the only way to reach him was to leave a message, and he would return the call when it was convenient.

Afterwards, he'd stripped, ready for a shower, when he'd noticed a little black electronic button attached to his trousers. Of course, he'd recognised the bug straight away, and he'd known who planted it on him.

For the first time in his adult life, he'd lost his temper. The humiliation had transformed to rage. He'd wanted to get his hands on the bloody woman and squeeze the life out of her.

Instead, after pacing and cursing for a few minutes, he'd dressed and gone to find Dapo. The man confirmed it was possible to trace the bug receiver synced to the transmitter by reverse-engineering computer wizardry.

While Kojo had been waiting for Dapo to get back to him, Razi had called. Kojo had explained the situation. He'd also forwarded the photo of the woman he'd taken. Razi's team would search their databases and Interpol's for any matches.

He'd fallen asleep close to dawn—about an hour in an armchair while he waited for an update from Razi or Dapo.

This morning, the big break had come via Dapo, who'd found the matching signal to the transmitter somewhere in Festac Town.

The exact location Kojo and Luke were heading to right now.

Luke slowed the SUV when they entered a quiet street. "The house we want is just down there according to the satnav."

"Okay. We're going to scout the area and the exterior of the premises before we do anything else," Kojo said and exited the vehicle.

One thing military training engraved in him was never to go into any situation blind. There were too many unknown variables, so they had to take precautions.

First, would someone kidnap a royal princess and remain in the same region like nothing had happened? Wouldn't they be lying low?

Then again, he remembered the woman who had palmed his dick in broad daylight. Her daring brown eyes had indicated she was up for anything. So perhaps she was bold enough to try hiding in plain sight after committing a criminal offence punishable by death.

In which case, this could be a hideout. If Kojo went charging into the premises to grab her, he could be walking into a trap.

He patted the grey jacket he wore over the black t-shirt and black jeans, confirming the handgun was in the shoulder holster. Along with the spare magazines in the pocket clips.

The street was primarily residential two-level houses surrounded by high concrete fences.

The building they needed was in a middle plot, so there was only one exit. Unless the target spotted them and jumped the back fence into the neighbour's compound.

The gate was locked.

Not wanting to spook anyone, they returned to the vehicle and sat there after scouting the area. Tricky to figure a way to gain entrance without attracting attention or alerting the kidnappers. They needed to capture the culprits alive so they could question them and locate the princess.

Afterwards, Kojo would make them all suffer for what they'd done.

He remembered the woman, and his hands balled into fists. Oh, he would make her pay.

A white Toyota Corolla pulled up outside the building.

"Something is about to go down," Luke said.

"Yeah. Stay alert." Kojo left the car with Luke.

They approached the car on both sides.

Kojo knocked on the front window, and the man wound down.

"Are you my pickup?" the man in the driver's seat asked.

"Who are you?" Kojo asked.

"Uber. Are you the passenger?" the man asked, looking from him to Luke.

Kojo ignored the question and asked another. "What is the destination?"

"The airport." The man looked at his phone on the dashboard. "Did you not book a cab? I have this address."

"Sorry. We thought you were someone else," Luke said.

Kojo indicated and moved to one side of the entrance while Luke went to the other.

Scuffing sounds and footsteps indicated someone inside was approaching the gates. Seconds later, the pedestrian hatch opened, and a woman stepped out, dragging a small case on rollers.

Her hair was long and curly, and she wore a black embroidered mid-length caftan over navy skinny jeans matched with black thigh-high boots with metal panels down the sides. She looked nothing like the cleaner Kojo had met yesterday. The shape of her face looked different, especially with the round, navy-rimmed glasses, making her look bookish.

Disappointment made Kojo's stomach clench because this could be another dead end.

Then the woman lifted her head in Kojo's direction. Something flickered in her gaze quickly and was gone.

It was her!

She jumped into the backseat of the car and shouted. "Go!"

The driver hesitated, allowing Kojo to stomp across the pavement and yank the door before she could close it.

"Get out." He reached for her.

"Driver, go! These men are trying to kidnap me," she screeched.

Pissed off, Kojo grabbed her arm and dragged her out of the car.

Like a hellcat, she fought him, kicking, clawing. But he was larger, more robust. The confined space didn't give her room to fight back. As soon as she was out, she swung her arm, bashing his head with her handbag.

Pain exploded in his skull. There must be something hard in it.

The rush of adrenaline helped him shake off the pain. He hauled her through the gates she'd exited, yelling over his shoulders to Luke. "Get rid of the Uber."

They didn't need an audience for what was coming next.

The woman was a wildcat. As he carried her into the premises, she clawed and kicked him in the groin. Pain watered his eyes.

"Bitch." He slammed her against the wall, gripping her throat in a chokehold while he tried to breathe through the ache. He clamped his legs around hers to stop her from lashing out again.

Her soft curves felt familiar, although they'd only spent minutes in intimate company yesterday. He'd imagined getting lost in her feminine charms. Meanwhile, she'd been setting him up for an abduction.

"Where is the princess?" he gritted out, snatching her bag, and dumping it on the ground in case she had a weapon in there.

"Who?" Her voice was raspy because his hand on her throat was rough and tight. Still, her eyes glared daggers.

He'd never manhandled a woman before. It wasn't in his nature to hurt people. But this one was a criminal. And the princess's life was at stake. Never mind his.

"Don't play dumb with me. Is she in there?" He tilted his head towards the two-storey building and loosened the grip on her throat so she could breathe and speak.

She coughed and panted.

"I don't know what you're talking about. There's no one in there. But feel free to search the house if you want." She sneered at him, although she stopped struggling.

He squashed his body against hers so she didn't have wiggle room and pulled a plastic zip tie from his pocket. Then he gripped both her hands with one of his and snapped the restraints on tight.

Luke entered the driveway. "The Uber is gone. I told him we were law enforcement here to arrest her. He seemed to buy it. But we have to hurry in case he calls the police."

"Impersonating a police officer is a crime, you know. So, you better let me go," the woman said.

"Shut up," Kojo replied, shoving her towards the front entrance. "Open the door."

"I can't. The keys are under the rock. Let me get it." She nodded towards the corner of the building where a potted plant stood next to decorative stones.

"Luke, find the keys." He wasn't taking any chances by letting her do it. She could have a weapon hidden there.

Luke walked over, moved the large terracotta pot, and pulled out a key in a metal ring. He walked to the door and slotted it in, twisting it until there was a clicking sound.

"Be careful," Kojo said. "It could be booby-trapped. Let her go first."

Pulling his handgun out, he shoved the woman. "Don't try anything, or I will shoot you."

She rolled her eyes heavenwards. "We both know you're not going to shoot me. If you wanted to kill me, you would have done so already."

Her response was the confirmation he needed. She wouldn't have spoken if she didn't feel she had leverage. She was the woman who had abducted Princess Isha, even if she looked different from the one who had seduced him. However, she was right.

She was the only lead they had to find the princess, so he needed her alive.

"It doesn't mean I don't want to cause you pain." He shoved her again, and she stumbled forward.

"A sadist, huh?" She winked as she recovered her posture and walked confidently, hips swaying provocatively. "As long as you're the one causing the pain, I'm here for it."

What the fuck? Was this woman for real? Was she turning this encounter into some kind of BDSM fetish?

She pushed the door and entered the house.

Luke glanced at Kojo, a knowing smile on his face.

Kojo's anger flamed, heating his cheeks. His colleague knew the woman had seduced him yesterday, which was how he'd lost the princess.

He stomped into the house behind her, gun still pointed at her head. "Luke, check out the rooms."

It was best to stay close to the woman in case she tried anything. He couldn't afford to lose her a second time.

The place was furnished lightly—one leather sofa and wooden coffee table—but had the musty and chemically smell of a residence not used frequently.

She stood in the middle of the living room, looking smug.

Luke came back. "Downstairs is clear. I'll check upstairs."

Kojo's heart raced. From the self-assured expression on her face, he knew the princess wasn't here. Luke wouldn't find anyone else upstairs.

"Where is she?" he asked again. His fingers flexed around the trigger. "You set me up. Seduced me so you could get access to the princess."

She didn't say anything, and he continued. "We found the laundry service owner and the cash you left. We also found the burnt-out van and the bug you planted on me."

That got a reaction out of her. Her eyes widened.

"Yes, we found the van and the bug. And we found you. So, it's only a matter of time before we find your accomplices. Do yourself a favour. Lead us to them and the princess. And I'll make sure your life is spared."

She laughed harshly, but it didn't reach her eyes.

"You're even more of a fool if you think I'm afraid of death. Bring it," she taunted, lips thin and tight, chin raised in defiance.

"Unh!" he growled. He would have put a bullet through her leg just to injure and inflict pain. But he wasn't sure she wouldn't bleed to death, and he couldn't waste time taking her to a hospital.

"There's no one here," Like said when he returned.

"We'll take her back to base. Kenny can extract the information we need from her," Kojo said. "Out."

Interestingly she walked out of the door without hesitating. Kojo followed while Luke locked up.

Kojo held her to his side, gun concealed so that nosy passers-by didn't notice as they walked to their dark SUV parked on the street.

Luke held the back door open.

"Get in and move over," Kojo said.

She didn't argue and obeyed.

Kojo slid in beside her, keeping the gun on her in case she tried to do anything.

Luke shut the door after him and went to the driver's seat. Soon afterwards, they left the vicinity as the sounds of sirens filled the air.

"Good thing we got out of there. It seems the cab driver called the police," Luke said.

The woman smirked, turning to look out of the window.

Kojo just fumed. "What is your name? And don't tell me it's Grace. We found the real Grace Bello."

"There are more than one Grace Bello on this planet." She replied, still not looking at him.

He snorted. "Yeah, right. You're not one of them. Anyway, we'll run your prints, and I'm sure you're on the Interpol list."

She swivelled, glaring at him. "What is really eating you? Are you more upset that I seduced you or that your precious princess got stolen from right under your nose?"

His anger flared again. "Fuck you!"

"I'd like that very much. Because if it's the former, I can make up for it right here. I will blow your mind like you've never had before." She placed her bound palms on Kojo's thigh and covered his junk.

His eyes widened as he caught her meaning.

"What?" He jerked away with a gasp as heat flooded him for all the wrong reasons and his dick filled involuntarily.

"Oh, come on. Has no one ever given you a blow job in the back seat of a car?"

He turned away, refusing to look at her as his cheeks flamed. She was playing mind games, and he refused to play along.

"No wonder you're so uptight," she continued. "There's nothing like it. It's even more fun when you're the one driving, and someone is going down on you. Am I right, Luke? Tell him."

He was part-horrified and part-aroused by the imagery, which was even more annoying considering the woman didn't even want him and was only taunting.

Luke glanced at him in the rear-view mirror and shrugged with a smirk.

Had the man done the same thing, getting head while driving?

It was just plain crazy. Something Kojo would never contemplate. He shook his head and glared at the woman. "You're crazy. Don't touch me again, or I will tie your hand to the headrest."

"Oh, bondage. I like. You're getting more intriguing by the minute. First, it was pain, now bondage. I'm here for it." She raised her bound wrists, her bottom lip tucked in at the corner in a suggestive gesture.

He stared at her luscious lips, remembered the taste of her and suppressed a groan.

Get a grip, man. She's trying to fuck with you.

"Just keep away from me." He growled and turned away, staring out of the window.

She laughed, the sound rich and warm and goddamned sexy.

Like a drug in his vein, his heart raced, and his dick filled. Why the hell was his body betraying him?

In the front, he could swear Luke was laughing, although it wasn't loud.

Kojo kicked the back of the driver's seat. "Don't you dare laugh as well."

"Whatever you say," Luke commented in an amused tone.

The rest of the drive to the hotel was in silence.

Kojo tried to figure out how he would make the woman talk and give up the location of the princess. If she intended to fly out of the country this afternoon, perhaps her accomplices were also catching the same flight.

From their information, there were at least two other people—the van driver and the man who had stayed with the hostages at the laundry premises.

It would be good to send men to the airport just to look out for suspicious behaviour at least and see if they could find any of the men fitting the descriptions they had.

He called Kenny and updated him. The other man agreed about sending men to the airport, both the domestic and international airports.

"Mr Doona wants to see you once you get back," Kenny said.

"Doona wants to see me? Why?" Kojo said.

The woman by his side stiffened. Did she know Kweku Doona? Was Kweku involved in the princess's kidnapping? It wasn't farfetched. The man was a sleazeball.

"Yes," Kenny's voice cut through his thoughts. "I told him you were out following a lead, and he said he wants you to see him as soon as you get back."

"Okay. I'll speak to him soon. We're not far from the hotel now."

"Alright, see you shortly."

"Hang on." Kojo stared at the woman. "Don't tell him about the latest development."

If Kweku was involved in the kidnapping, Kojo didn't want him knowing that one of the accomplices had been found. He needed to know what was going on first.

"Sure," Kenny replied and hung up.

Not long after, Luke drove the car into the hotel car park.

"Is the Doona bastard here?" the woman asked in a grim tone.

Kojo was tempted to ignore her question, but he was more curious about why she was asking. For the first time since they captured her, she seemed on the defensive.

"Do you know Kweku Doona?" he asked, turning to her.

"Who doesn't?" she retorted.

"What do you know about him?"

"I know that you shouldn't tell him who I am."

"Why?"

"Can I talk to you one-to-one?" She glanced at Luke, who was still sitting in front.

"Why should I trust you?" Kojo watched her body language, trying to gauge any deception.

"You shouldn't. But I have something just for your ears only."

He didn't' trust her. But something had changed inside her once Doona's name dropped into the equation. He wanted to know why? Also, it seemed she didn't like Doona anyway since she'd called him 'bastard'.

"Luke, excuse us for a minute," Kojo said.

Nodding, Luke stepped out and shut the door.

"I'm all ears," Kojo said, giving his full attention.

"Look," she started, twisting in her seat to face him. "I know this whole situation is hard on you."

He stiffened, glaring at her. "You have no clue what's hard on me."

She raised her hands in a conciliatory gesture. "Whatever. But I can help you."

"Help me, how?"

"I can take you to the princess."

His heart raced. He wanted that, but he didn't trust her. She was trying to trick him again. "All of a sudden, you can take me to the princess. Why now?"

"Isn't that what all this is about. You want to see the princess and know she is okay. You want to rescue her, don't you?"

More than anything else. "Yes."

"But if you hand me over to Kweku Doona, he will torture me to get answers. It will take days, and you will be no closer to finding the princess because I won't talk. I'd rather die than tell him anything. And the situation will be out of your control. I can't imagine the good people of the Kingdom of Bagumi will be happy that you lost their princess. I know your life will be forfeit if she never returns."

He stiffened, his anger flaring. Stowing his weapon in his holster, he reached for the door.

"Wait." She touched his shoulder, her palm branding his skin.

He stared at her hand, glaring. "I told you not to touch me."

"I'm sorry." She raised her hands. "Can you not see beyond your ego? I'm trying to save you."

"My ego? How dare you? You're the reason I'm in this mess in the first place." He clenched his hands to stop from strangling her.

"I know it's my fault, and I want to make it up to you." Her voice was soft, enticing.

"By taking me to her."

"Yes."

"And what's in it for you."

"Freedom. You don't tell the Doona shit who I am, and you don't hand me over to anyone else. In return, I'll take you to the princess. Just you and me."

"Just you and me. You'll take me to her today."

"Well, it will take more than a day to get to her."

"Where is she?"

"She's not in Nigeria anymore."

His heart clenched, and he wrapped his hand around her neck, yanking her close. "I hope you didn't hurt her."

"No. We didn't hurt her." She rasped, choking on his grip as she tried to claw at his hand.

He loosened his grip but didn't release her. "Where is she?"

"I can't tell you." She coughed.

He growled and released her. "Fine. We'll catch a flight to wherever you were going."

He grabbed her bag from the front seat where Luke had put it and pulled out the airline ticket. "Accra. You were going to Accra? Is that where she is?"

If the princess was in Accra, then he might be in luck. He was half-Ghanaian and had family there. So, he could get local help.

She rubbed her neck and shrugged. "We can't take a flight out of here anyway. Thanks to you threatening me, the uber driver reported you. So now the police are looking for you and me, probably at the airports. We can't fly."

"Good point. Then we're going on a road trip."

"Yay." She said without enthusiasm.

He looked at the name on the ticket. Leyna Jakande. He doubted it was her real name.

"Tell me your name," he said in a quiet voice.

"You can read, can't you?"

He threw the ticket back in the bag. "That is not your real name. You're not Nigerian."

Although she spoke fluent English, instinct said she wasn't local. And her knowledge of Kweku Doona made him suspect she could be Wanaian.

"If we're going to do this, then I need to know the real name of the person I'm working with. You must give me something. Also, I need verification that what you are saying is true."

She puffed out air. "Fine. My real name is Latifah. But it's for your ears alone."

"Latifah what?"

"I'm not willing to divulge that at this moment."

"Bu—" he was going to say 'bullshit', but she interrupted.

"Here is information you can verify. A private aeroplane departed MMA and landed in Tambao, Burkina Faso late last night."

He glared at her, and she held his gaze without flinching.

"If you try to trick me again or give me false information, the deal is off, and I will hand you over to the authorities."

"Fair enough." She shrugged.

He opened the door and stepped outside.

"What was that about?" Luke asked.

"We'll talk about it later at the team briefing. But, for now, you can take a break and get some lunch."

"No probs."

Kojo walked over to Latifah's side and opened the door while pulling the penknife from his pocket. "Raise your hands."

She lifted her bound hands, and he flicked the blade and sliced the tie off.

"Thank you," she murmured as she rubbed her wrists.

"Now, walk normally. Don't try anything. Or I will shoot you. And before you think I'm bluffing, I'm an excellent marksman. I can hit you in the butt even while you're in motion."

A huff was her only response.

Kojo and Luke walked into the hotel, flanking Latifah, who dragged the small suitcase. To anyone, she looked like a hotel guest or one of the security team. None of the staff they went past seemed to recognise her.

With the change of clothes, hair, and makeup, she looked like a different person.

"I'll see you later." Luke headed towards the restaurant.

Kojo opened the door to the security suite and waved for Latifah to enter. Since they had an ongoing case at the hotel, the Cruz team maintained the conference room.

"Welcome back," Dapo eyed Latifah when they entered. "How did it go?"

"We'll talk in a minute. I need to find Mr Doona." Kojo took the suitcase from Latifah and shoved it into a corner.

Dapo pointed at the monitors. "He's in the swimming area."

"Okay. Thanks. Check for any flights that departed Lagos last night and landed in Burkina Faso. Tambao specifically." Kojo swivelled to leave.

"Will do. Do you need me to secure her?" Dapo asked.

"No. She's staying with me. I'll see you later." He held onto Latifah's elbow and steered her down the corridor towards the swimming pool.

He couldn't leave her with anyone else. He didn't trust anyone but himself to keep an eye on her. Although she had promised to take him to the princess, he didn't trust her not to run if given the opportunity.

At the poolside, he spotted Kweku in the pool frolicking with a woman Kojo didn't recognise. The man was back to his old tricks. He didn't look like a man who was mourning the loss of his abducted fiancée.

Pissed, Kojo stomped to the edge of the paving slabs.

"Mr Doona, you wanted to see me," he said in an imperious tone.

Kweku pushed the woman away and swivelled. His guilt was written all over his face. He swam to the edge of the pool and climbed up the steps.

"Yes, Kojo. I was told you went to check out a new lead," he said in his usual pompous tone as he grabbed a towel from a sun-lounger.

"We found an address that we thought was used as a hideout, but when we arrived, they had all gone. So, it's another dead-end." Kojo usually didn't tell lies. But he was loath to tell Kweku any new information, considering what he'd just seen the man doing. Kweku could go do his own damned investigation if he really wanted to find Princess Isha.

The dishonourable man did not deserve the royal.

Plus, Latifah had been correct about Kweku. If Kojo told him who Latifah was, the man would detain Latifah and take over the investigation. Kojo would be dismissed.

Also, he didn't want to share sensitive information in public.

"Okay. Keep me updated." Kweku waved him away as the bikini-clad woman approached.

"Of course." Clenching his fist, Kojo swivelled and walked away with Latifah in tow.

He headed for the lift lobby. Time to plan for the upcoming trip.

Chapter 7

"I need to make a phone call," Latifah said as they waited for the lifts.

"No," Kojo replied, still pissed off about Kweku. He wasn't about to give Latifah liberties either. She was manipulative. He couldn't forget that. She probably intended to lead him on a wild goose chase.

"If I don't check-in, they will think that something happened to me," she said in a conversational tone. "Who knows what they will do to your princess."

He swivelled, stepped up to her, glaring. He didn't think he'd dealt with this much anger all his life.

Standing this close to her, he could see the flecks of gold in determined her eyes, the sensual bow of her lips. The musk of her perfume was intoxicating.

His arousal pulsed to life, mixing with his anger. "Are you threatening me?"

"It's not a threat. Just a statement of fact. I'm due for a check-in." She didn't even flinch, as composed as ever.

If she was due to check-in, he had to allow her to make the phone call. To not alert her accomplices into moving or harming the princess until Kojo got her out of there.

"Fine. You can make the call when we get upstairs." He jabbed his finger on the lift call button.

"No. Your room might be bugged. I want to do it outside where there's less chance of being recorded or traced."

He opened his mouth to refute, but she placed a hand on his chest, cutting off his words and his breath. "You can stay with me and listen to what I say if you like. I just don't want anyone else overhearing."

"And if I say no."

"Then I won't make the call."

He glared, grabbed her elbow, and dragged her towards a side door leading to the gardens.

Outside, he said, "Make the call."

She withdrew a phone from the pocket of her trousers, inserted a tiny sim card into the device and fiddle with the keypad.

His gaze stayed on her as she raised the gadget to her ear and spoke rapidly. "It's me. Can't chat for long. I got delayed but will be crossing soon. There are no birds on the wire, but there are more dogs and fences. Also, I've got a guide so I should be fine. We'll see you soon."

She clicked another button, dismantled the gadget, taking the sim out.

"Give it to me." He extended his hand.

Arching out of reach, she snapped the chip in half and dumped it and the device into his palm.

"Uh," he growled, glaring from the useless sim to her.

She shrugged. "Sorry."

The apology rankled. She didn't appear one bit sorry.

He balled his hands into fists, the gadget digging into his palm. He could grab her neck and squeeze the life out of her.

Still, it wouldn't bring him any closer to finding HRH.

He exhaled and opened his hand, reassembling the phone.

The call had lasted less than ten seconds and mainly sounded like code. Nothing was incriminating. Nothing to identify the caller or the listeners. Maybe he could find a traceable number on the device.

It was an old model phone, probably a burner, only suitable for making phone calls or sending text messages. No internet service. It was the kind of phone someone would use if they didn't want to be tracked or hacked.

He clicked the button to check the contacts, but there was no entry. Zero. And her call log was empty too. She'd deleted the one she'd just made.

"Who are you?" He asked in exasperation, handing the phone over to her.

Her actions were familiar. Like something Razi would do. But his brother was a covert agent. Was Latifah a spy too?

She returned the device to her pocket and invaded his personal space. Her brown eyes sparkled, her luscious lips curling at the corners.

"That's for you to find out. We'll have plenty of time to discover each other on the road trip."

Her tone was soft and full of innuendo. She was teasing again like she'd done in the car.

Pulse rate spiking, he glanced away. They weren't far from the spot where she'd bumped into him with the trolley yesterday.

At the time, he'd thoughted he'd scored lucky. After the way she'd propositioned him, he'd assumed they would spend the night together in pleasurable ways. Instead, she'd turned into a nightmare.

Emotions unfamiliar and old punched through him. He always seemed to be on the defensive while she was the aggressor.

Even knowing the dangers she posed, he was still attracted to her. He couldn't lie to himself.

Yes, he hated this desire for her, which clouded his judgement. This craving fizzing in his veins, making him itch to crush her body against the wall and seal their lips together. Making him want to hear her whisper his name in ecstasy. Making him want to drive into her welcoming wet heat again and again until they were both sated.

He hated her, damn it.

And yet, he didn't. How could he be attracted to someone he hated?

He grabbed her shoulder, tugged her until she crashed into his chest.

"The only reason I want to know you is so I can find the princess," he gritted out and waved at the door. "Let's go."

"Whatever you say." She shook her head and entered the corridor.

He snorted. He wouldn't be stupid enough to believe she would be so compliant. She wanted to get rid of him as much as he needed to find the princess.

The phone in his pocket rang, and he pulled it out.

"Are you free for a briefing?" Kenny asked when the call connected.

"I'm on my way," Kojo said and hung up.

"This way," he said to Latifah when they reached the lobby and directed her back to the security suite.

Luke, Dapo and Kenny were already there. They stared at Latifah as she walked in, looking as if they were intrigued by her presence.

Kojo pointed at a chair in the far corner and said to Latifah. "Go and sit over there."

She sashayed across smoothly, ignoring the men as she went past. They all watched her swivel and lower her body onto the chair before crossing her legs and staring right back at them.

She was as bold as fuck. He'd give her that. She showed zero shame or remorse.

Kojo walked to the round table in the middle of the room and pulled out a chair. The other men followed his lead and settled around the table.

"So, what's the update on the hideout?" Kojo asked, wanting to divert attention from the woman.

Kenny spoke first. "My contact in law enforcement said they weren't able to get any usable fingerprints or DNA. The place was thoroughly sterilised. The owner said someone from a company registered in Liberia made the reservations for the house and car for the week. Sunday was supposed to be the last day of the booking. The name was Leyna Jakande."

Kojo stiffened. He knew that name.

"It's also the name that came up when I ran the checks on the private flight from MMA, which landed in Tambao last night," Dapo said. "The flight manifest indicated there had been a woman and three men on board as well as the crew. Supposedly a businessman, his wife, and their bodyguards. The flight had been booked by a company in Liberia, the same Leyna person. The ground crew who saw them board said the woman had been in a red ballgown similar to what HRH was wearing yesterday."

"That's good news. A positive sighting." Hope flared in Kojo's heart. The princess had been alive when she'd arrived in Burkina Faso. A private flight meant she'd had some comfort even though she was a captive. Perhaps her captors would not be cruel to her.

He glanced at Latifah. She had an I-told-you-so smirk on her face. He looked away.

"It's good news. But do we know who this Leyna Jakande is? The name sounds Nigeria," Kenny said.

"The name is not showing up on any lists, and I can't find her on social media," Dapo replied.

"What about the company?" Kojo asked, wanting to get all the facts before he told them about Latifah.

"It seems to be a dummy corporation. The transactions keep pinging all over the place, from Mauritius to Djibouti to Liberia, so it's difficult to track where the original money came from. And it seemed the credit card used for the property booking was cloned. Although it wasn't charged since the property owner was paid by cash in full at the start of the reservation. The person who paid him was Leyna Jakande."

Kojo glanced at Latifah again. She and her associates had cloned someone's credit card. How many other people had they duped? The good thing being they hadn't defrauded the person by charging to the card.

She shrugged as if to say it couldn't be helped.

How could she be so blasé?

He frowned before facing the men. "She is Leyna Jakande."

"Her?" Kenny asked, staring at Latifah.

"Yes. She conspired with her accomplices to abduct HRH."

"So why isn't she locked up? Why aren't we interrogating her?" Kenny asked.

"Good question." Kojo sighed, scrubbing palms over his face. "I'd lock her up and throw away the key. But she has proven to be cooperative. She gave us the flight details, which has been verified. So, we know where the princess was taken. Leyna has promised to take me to the exact location."

"And you trust her to do as she says?" Dapo chimed in.

"No, I don't trust her. But we have few other options. Interrogation will not necessarily yield any more information that we have. It will also take time. Meanwhile, the princess remains a captive. But if I go with her, then there is a likelihood of seeing the princess sooner rather than later."

"Did she tell you why they took HRH? Is there a ransom demand?" Luke asked.

"No and no. Not yet anyway."

"I don't trust her," Kenny said in a stiff tone. "She manipulated you before. She could be doing it again."

"You know I'm right here, and I can hear you guys, right?" Latifah said in a bored tone before Kojo could reply.

He groaned as the other men turned towards her.

"Luke," she continued. "How about we leave the others to chat while we find ways of entertaining ourselves. Do you have a room here? We could go and Netflix—"

Kojo didn't let her finish. "Shut the fuck up!"

The flare of his temper was sudden but not unexpected. He'd been ebbing and flowing on a tide of anger since this woman entered his life and the princess vanished.

"What did I say?" She tried to look innocent.

Did she have no shame? Yesterday she'd invited him to Netflix and chill. Today she was asking his colleague.

Kojo would not fall for the ruse again. Not to mention how much it cut him open and made his heart bleed because she would offer her body to his colleague even in jest. It was irrational to make any claim on her. Still, he couldn't seem to help the emotions roiling inside him.

"If you say one more word, I will gag you," he threatened in a stern voice.

It seemed to work because she used hand gestures to zip her mouth. She threw an imaginary key away and leaned back into the seat, arms crossed over her chest. Still, the smirk remained on her face. As if she wasn't truly convinced or wanted to dare him anyway.

Yet it felt like she was trying to save his face in front of his colleagues, which seemed weirder. Why would she try to keep him from embarrassment?

He sucked in calming breaths before facing the other men, using the interlude to remember what they had discussed before the interruption.

"As I said earlier, I don't trust her," he continued. "But finding the princess promptly and intact is of topmost priority to her family and me. So, I have to take this chance."

"I agree," Dapo said. "This is the best chance we have, so far, of getting HRH back."

"I think so too," Luke added.

"Fine," Kenny conceded. "If you're going with her, I supposed Luke can go with you."

"No." Kojo shook his head. "The deal is that it will be me alone with her. No one else."

Kenny frowned and tilted his head as he stood.

Kojo followed him as they stepped outside the room and shut the door.

"Are you sure you want to do that?" Kenny asked in a low voice.

"It's the best option we have," Kojo replied. "I don't want to spook her. She has given us vital traceable information so far."

"But if you don't have backup she can lure you into an ambush."

"Yes. That's why we'll keep some form of communication. There's the tracker on the car and the electronic devices. So, you'll know where we are. Luke can follow in another vehicle at a safe distance."

"Okay. We'll do that."

"One more thing. Mr Doona. Explain to him that I'm away chasing a new lead and will be unreachable for a few days."

"No problem."

"I'll leave you to brief Luke. I need to go upstairs and pack up."

Kojo walked into the office and said, "Time to go."

"See you around, gentlemen." Latifah stood and sashayed out of the security suite, dragging her carry-on luggage.

Kojo walked a step behind until they reached the lobby. He grabbed her elbow, punched the button to call the lift. It beeped and opened immediately. In the boxcar, they stood side by side, facing the door. Her proximity made his skin tingle. He focused on regulating his breathing. Yet, her zesty fragrance—had to be orange blossoms—tickled his nostrils.

When the lift pinged and opened, he stepped out first, needing the smell anything else but her. They walked past room 4-0-7, and he remembered her in the cleaner's uniform standing there, staring at him.

Shaking his head, he shoved the memory away and unlocked the princess's suite. Sunshine flooded into the suite from the uncovered glass windows. He held the door.

Latifah sashayed in. She left her suitcase in the hallway and entered the living area. "This is nice."

"Sit and don't touch anything." He pointed at an armchair.

Not speaking, she walked over and settled in.

Kojo busied himself, packing Princess Isha's belongings. He called Kenny to book a courier to send the luggage to Bagumi. There was no point keeping the items here.

One, the princess was no longer in Nigeria and would not be returning here. Two, they had booked the rooms until tonight, anyway. Even if he extended the booking, he would not be here, so safer to send them home.

Kojo's phone buzzed, and he pulled it out of his pocket to read the message from Reggie, Princess Amara's personal bodyguard.

Princess Amara is on her way to you.

Shit. Kojo didn't want her coming in here and seeing Latifah. But before he could do anything, a knock sounded on the suite door.

"Don't move from that chair," he reiterated before walking to the door and unlocking it.

The Nigerian princess stood there with Reggie behind her, looking dishevelled. Under normal circumstances, she would be immaculately presented, not a strand of hair out of place. He'd known her for nine years and had never seen a crease on her face or rumple in her clothing.

Now, she wore grey and pink sneakers, grey sports legging, a black tank top and her long hair looped in a messy bun. With slumped shoulders, no makeup on her face, worry lines and puffy eyes, this was the most unkempt he'd seen her.

However, these were not normal circumstances.

Her best friend was missing, and Kojo was responsible. Protecting people was the one thing he was supposed to be good at, and he'd messed up spectacularly.

"Princess, is there something I can do?" he asked in a gentle voice, body feeling weighted with a heavy load.

"I'd like an update. Can I come in?" Amara's voice was low and croaky.

"Sure." He moved out of the way, so she walked past him. Reggie stayed outside as Kojo shut the door.

"Oh," Amara halted in the middle of the living room when she saw Latifah sitting in the armchair. "I'm sorry. I didn't know you were busy."

"It's not a problem." Heat flashed up Kojo's neck in annoyance. The princess probably assumed he and Latifah were lovers or something. "The lady is just helping us with enquiries. We can talk over here."

Latifah didn't say anything, thankfully, and he didn't bother introducing her to the princess. Nothing good could come from connecting the two—the abductor and the victim's friend—in a casual manner. It would be cruel and improper.

Instead, he guided Amara into the small open-plan high-gloss kitchenette and pulled out a stool at the bar.

"I can't sit still," she said and walked around the bar towards the kitchen counter. She went through the motion of spooning fresh ground coffee into the filter and setting up the machine to brew.

An ache bloomed in Kojo's throat, and his heartbeat slowed.

One of the many things Isha and Amara shared—the love for fresh coffee. It was a ritual for them whenever they were together, brewing, drinking, chatting.

The two had been friends longer than Kojo had been guarding Isha.

Watching Amara go through the motions reminded him how much he'd messed up. He curled his palms into fists instead of rubbing his painful chest. He fought to maintain control. Amara needed his composure. His strength. More to the point, she needed her friend back, healthy, and safe.

"What's the news?" she turned and leaned against the counter, arms crossed on her midriff. "I know you went out this morning. Reggie said you were following a lead."

Kojo blinked in surprise. He hadn't expected her to know of his whereabouts. Still, it made sense she would want to be updated.

Sighing, he climbed onto a stool, using the motion to gather his thoughts. He couldn't reveal Latifah's actual involvement because it would prompt more questions he couldn't answer. And he couldn't tell Amara more than he'd told Kweku, fearing the two would discuss the situation and swap notes.

Kweku wasn't beyond using underhand methods to further his aims, including using Isha's grieving friend as an inadvertent spy.

"Yes, I went out earlier. We had a tip about a possible hideout for the people who took..." he trailed off, unable to complete the sentence as his throat clogged up. He needed to keep it together. "Anyway, it was a dead end."

Amara's face fell, and her eyes became glassy. She swivelled and took a cup from the counter. She poured black coffee into it, brought it over and placed it on the counter. "You can have this. Have you eaten? You probably missed breakfast and lunch since you went out early."

Amara's need to keep busy was another sign of her distress, which tore at him.

He understood the urge to keep moving. Any action was better than staying still while Princess Isha was out there, in an unknown situation.

"No. I haven't eaten," he replied, wrapping fingers around the white porcelain cup. "But don't worry about it."

He hadn't eaten since before the party last night. He'd only had coffee on the go this morning.

"Nonsense." She opened the fridge and withdrew a large cream plate stacked with cupcakes. "I bought this for us to share today. You know Isha. She hates waste. So, you might as well eat it."

She took smaller plates from the cupboard, served cakes onto them, and brought one to him.

"Would your friend like one?" Amara asked, looking over his shoulder.

Friend? Kojo followed her gaze to where Latifah sat in the living area about four metres away. She watched them with a blank expression.

Glaring, he opened his mouth to say the woman wasn't his friend, could never be his friend after what she'd done. But he closed it.

Mentioning the animosity between him and Latifah would stir questions from Amara. Questions he couldn't answer. As much as he despised the woman, he was bound to the deal he'd made with Latifah. He couldn't give her a reason to renege, although he didn't believe she wouldn't abscond if given the opportunity.

Amara was correct about Isha loathing wastage. The food would end in the bin if not eaten. And he would get an earful from the royal when she found out. Then again, did he want to feed her kidnapper?

His temples throbbed with a looming headache. He was overthinking the situation.

Not feeding Latifah wouldn't bring Isha back any sooner.

He grabbed the plate and the coffee cup, walked over to Latifah, placing them on the small dark wood table beside her. "Here."

"I don't want any," Latifah said in a tight whisper.

Anger flared inside him. He lowered his head to her ear and said in a low menacing tone. "She gave you the cake. So, eat the damned cake. Or I swear—"

"Fine," she cut him off, gaze averted. He leaned back, narrowed his eyes, and glared at her until she said in a louder voice. "Thank you for the cake, princess."

"You're welcome," Amara replied.

Relaxing his expression, he returned to the breakfast counter where Amara had served more cakes and coffee for him.

"Sit." She indicated the stool as she pulled out another one opposite him.

He sat and waited for her to do the same. She lifted the mug in front of her and took a sip. Kojo took one of the cakes, unwrapped the paper and took a bite.

"We both developed a love for cupcakes when we were in London together." Amara stared into her mug with a forlorn expression. "There was this cake shop not far from where we lived. We would buy them by the dozens. They never lasted long, though." Her lips tugged up at the corner. "Our friends would show up. Even Zik used to come over just to eat cupcakes."

Kojo's mouth went dry, and he took sips of the black coffee to clear his throat. "Prince Zik?"

"Yes. He was in London with us for a year while he studied for his Master's degree." Her face brightened.

"Okay. I didn't realise. Was that where you and Princess Isha became friends?" he knew the story but wanted to keep her talking. It seemed to help her.

"No. Our families' friendship started before we were born. As children, we visited each other's homes. But it wasn't until we were in a Swiss boarding school together that we truly bonded and became tight friends."

She sipped coffee, bracing the mug in both hands. "Do you think her abduction has something to do with her political views?"

Kojo's face crumpled in a frown. "I don't think so. Why?"

"We were discussing the situation in Wanai yesterday. Isha is very passionate and vocal. She never sits on the fence on any topic. She hates any form of inequality or oppression and cares about the underdog. When we were students, she used to picket the embassies of countries under brutal regimes. These days, she's toned down a bit. But still ... I used to tease her that she could get into trouble because of her opinions. And I can't help wondering if an extremist group has targeted her because of it."

She puffed out a heavy breath as she stared into her mug like it would give her answers to Isha's whereabouts.

The idea of a group like Boko Haram abducting HRH sent a cold shiver down his spine. Latifah was hardly a poster model for BH with the body-con clothes and without the veil. However, it didn't mean she wasn't part of another extremist organisation.

Wanting to reassure Amara without making promises he couldn't keep, he reached across and placed a hand over hers on the mug.

She looked up, tears welling in her eyes. "You're going to find her, aren't you?"

The expression on her face was expectant as if he was the messiah. His guilt ramped up. If only he could go back to last night and undo everything.

"I'm going to try." A weak response but the best he could do.

"Oh, God." She dropped her head on the counter.

His heart tore in two, and he swallowed with difficulty. "We found out where they took her last night."

She lifted her head and swiped her face with the back of her hand. "Where?"

He reached for the box of tissues and passed them to her. "She was on a private plane landed in Burkina Faso last night. That's why I'm packing up. I'm heading over there."

"Oh, that's good." She wiped her face and chucked the used tissues in the bin. "What can I do?"

"It's okay." He pushed the plate with the half-eaten cupcake aside.

"No. Let me do something." She climbed off the stool. "I feel guilty enough because I organised the party. It was because of me that she got kidnapped."

Kojo stiffened, straightened. "You're not at fault here."

He was responsible. If he'd done his job well, they wouldn't be here.

"Well, it's how I feel. So let me do something. Please." Her chin was set with determination, and her eyes glassed over.

He understood her need to do something. He had the same urgency.

"Okay." He sighed. "I've packed her belongings and arranged for a courier to take them to Bagumi. If you can store them in your room until the courier arrives to pick them that would be great." He'd spent last night packing most of the items anyway.

"Yes. I can do that." She nodded.

"Thank you," he murmured.

They spent the next few minutes moving Princess Isha's luggage to Amara's room with Reggie's help.

However, Kojo kept her passport, phone, and other personal items with him for when he found her.

Almighty willing, he would find her.

Chapter 8

The day was not going Latifah's way.

Still, things could be a lot worse. She could be semi-conscious with a bullet hole in her gut, leaking blood while she crawled from a ditch, seeking rescue.

Grazing the old scar through her tunic with the heel of her palm, she offered up silent gratitude for life's mercies.

Being intercepted by Kojo on her way to the airport had been unforeseen and annoying. Still, she'd figured there would be opportunities to get away from him.

Until she'd overheard him mention Kweku Doona, and her rage had bubbled. It had been a game-changer. First, she'd thought Kojo would hand her over to the Wanaian president's son. She'd decided that if she got into Kweku's custody, she would kill him and face the consequences of her actions. Because she wouldn't have come out of his detention alive anyway.

She'd offered Kojo the deal because the alternatives were so much worse. Since Kojo hadn't resorted to the violence to restrain her, he'd been the lesser of two evils, so to speak. Not that she thought Kojo was evil. He'd been sweet yesterday.

Today, not so much. But he was angry, which was fair enough, considering what she'd done.

Sitting in his hotel suite listening to Princess Amara sob about the loss of her friend had been heart-rending. Latifah had felt like shit, still did, because she'd been the one to cause the distress.

When she'd planned the mission, she hadn't thought she would witness the aftermath of the abduction from the perspective of those left behind by the princess while they worried about her whereabouts.

She had no problems making evil people pay for their actions. However, she'd never sought to hurt innocent people. The reason for the mission was to prevent ordinary people from getting harmed.

Yet, she'd hurt Princess Isha's family and friends by taking her. She'd wounded Kojo by using him as a pawn and screwing up his job. The way he'd treated her so far showed he was one of the good guys, even if his charge, the princess of Bagumi, was engaged to an evil man.

Now Latifah wanted to make amends.

Hence she sat in the front passenger seat of the dark SUV. Kojo was driving along the Lagos-Badagry Expressway towards the border between Nigeria and Benin Republic. They'd left Goldcrest Hotel about two hours ago.

Kojo hadn't said much to her since they left the hotel. The hum of the air-conditioner blasted freezing air, filled the silence, and muted the sounds of the megacity whizzing past.

Regardless of the silence, it wasn't awkward. On the contrary, there was natural chemistry between them even with the animosity of their current situation.

Part of her wanted the easy conversationalist who'd flirted with her yesterday evening when she'd bumped into him with a laundry cart.

Yet, she understood he wouldn't treat her with such friendliness again.

He'd surprised her, though, by catching her at the safehouse. She'd assumed she'd be long gone before they discovered the place in Festac Town. That Dapo guy must be very good with technology to trace the bug's receiver in a short time.

A stupid mistake. One she wouldn't be making again.

In a way, she was glad to have his company for the international border crossings. They would travel through five countries before reaching their destination. Having Kojo, who had a diplomatic fast-track pass, would make it all go smoother.

Another hour and they drove through Badagry, which was the final point of departure for indigenes sold into transatlantic slavery between the 16th and 19th centuries. The town was also the site of the first European mission in Nigeria back in 1842.

The first border crossing was about an hour away, depending on traffic.

Kojo was dressed in the black t-shirt and jeans he'd been wearing when he'd turned up at the house. Underneath his lightweight black jacket was the holstered handgun.

Did he really plan to cross the land border with a concealed weapon that would be found in a quick body search? Even with his diplomatic ID, he would have to lock the gun in a case and show papers granting him a license to bear arms.

Of course, she wanted to avoid deep scrutiny. The less attention anyone paid her, the better.

"Are you going to try crossing the border with that gun on display?" she asked, glancing at him.

"What if I am?" he replied, but the slight curl of the lips proved he knew more than he was letting on. He knew that carrying the weapon would attract attention.

"Fine," she replied. He had as much to lose if they got delayed because of his weapon. So, she would play it cool for now.

There were other things he was keeping from her, like the vehicles trailing them.

Kojo had reneged on their arrangement. But she would give him the benefit of the doubt.

The first car had been following them for as long as they'd been on the road. She'd only noticed the second one in the last thirty minutes or so. Each time Kojo changed lanes, the vehicle did as well.

It only awakened the agent in her, whose instincts were trained to fight rather than flee. Kinda opposite to Kojo, who was skilled to be defensive and only react as protection. She was proficient at being on the offensive. To act first to prevent a situation from escalating.

She twisted the knob, changing the radio to a 90s RnB station, playing a Backstreet Boys song.

Old memories came back, and she started singing along to the track and swaying her body.

Kojo tilted his head to look at her strangely. "You know this song?"

"Of course." She shrugged. "I was a teenager in the 90s. Backstreet Boys were popular then, and my sister loved them."

An amazing thing happened. His lips curled upwards. He was actually smiling, even if it was tentative. The first time he'd smiled since yesterday. She wanted more of it.

"Your sister?" His voice rumbled with humour and hit her low in the belly. That gentle vibration was like kryptonite, turning her insides into lava.

"I think *you* had a thing for the band as well. You were just singing along to the lyrics. There I thought you were badass." Now he was taunting her.

Warmth spread through her that he thought she was badass. She wrinkled her nose. "I can be badass and like boybands. They are not mutually exclusive."

"I guess you can." He didn't seem eager to push it.

She wanted to keep him talking, to keep feeling the vibrations of his gentle rumble. If she was pressed against him while he was talking, would he induce an orgasm? Gosh, her mind always seemed to drift to sex when she was around him. Then again, he was her wet dream come to life. Did he have a steady lover at home? There was no mention in his file.

"So, is there a Mrs Kojo Hamadou?" she asked, sizing him up.

"How do you know my full name?" he glanced at her, eyes narrowed.

"Come on. Are you really going to ask me that?" She tilted her head.

He grimaced, and his lips tightened. "In which case, you should know the answer."

"Well, there was nothing in your dossier about a wife. Doesn't mean you don't have one squirrelled away somewhere in the middle of the back and beyond?"

He chuckled. The sound was surprisingly warm, considering he was still wary of her. Then he shook his head. "Do I look to you like the kind of person who would squirrel a wife away?"

"Actually, no, you don't." He was the serious sort. The kind of man who would commit himself fully to a spouse. The same way he was committed to his job. "But I had to ask."

"Why? It's not as if you are interested in me, anyway." He said the words flippantly, and the annoyance was back in his tone.

"You're right. I have no interest in being your wife. But I was curious, and we have unfinished business involving a night of sex." There was no point pretending there wasn't the attraction that needed to be burned off.

He coughed, raising one hand to cover his mouth as he glanced at her.

"Are you okay?" She smiled, amused at how easily she could tease him. He seemed so straightlaced that each time she mentioned sex, he seemed caught off-guard.

"I'm fine." He said when he composed himself. "We both know that's a lie too. You don't want to get into bed with me any more than you want to be my wife. So just stop taunting me. Anyway, what about you? Is there a Mr Latifah?"

She wanted to refute his claim about her not wanting him in her bed, but she let that go for now. She desired him. There was no faking it. Her sexy dream about him and the resulting orgasm was proof.

But she understood that all her deception and crimes had turned him off. So, for now, she focused on passing the time while they travelled.

"No. There's no Mr Latifah. My life doesn't support having a spouse."

"I suppose not. You can't very well tell your husband. 'Bye, hon. I'm off to work' when you go off to abduct people or declare 'ransoms' as your source of income."

She sucked in a deep breath to stop from retorting and revealing her real line of work. His words cut her unexpectedly. She'd never cared about what random people thought about her. The only people that mattered were the people she was fighting for—her family and her country.

"Touché," she said instead.

He didn't say anything. But his grip on the steering wheel tightened. Finally, after a few minutes, he asked in a low voice. "Is that really what you do for a living? Abducting and extorting money from people?"

"Does it matter what I do for a living? I'm the bad person, abductor of princesses." She curled her fingers in air quotes.

"Unh." He growled. "Don't bloody joke about this. This is not a joke. Do you not understand that her family is distressed about what you've done? Not to mention the trauma it might cause the princess. Or that you ruined my life."

Guilt pelted her skin. She was filled with remorse, especially regarding any distress to the princess's family.

"I wasn't trying to make a joke," she said in a sober tone. "I know the seriousness of my actions, and I'm sorry about the emotional stress caused."

"Really? You're sorry?"

"I am."

"So why do it?"

"I'm fighting for something bigger than me. Something worthwhile. For the greater good."

"What greater good?"

"You wouldn't understand."

"Why don't you try me?"

She sighed. "I can't tell you. For starters, I'm sworn to secrecy. Secondly, this car is bugged, and I know others are listening to this conversation."

"I don't know what you're talking about."

"Oh, don't pretend. Falsehoods are not you. I've been in this business long enough to expect worse."

"You're paranoid."

"No, I'm not. Two vehicles are tailing us."

"That's ridiculous."

She ignored him and continued. "I'm assuming one of them was sent by the Cruz team. But I wonder who the other one is. How deeply involved are the Nigerian authorities? I don't think the Bagumian crew would have arrived so quickly. But, oh..." she trailed off as a thought crossed her mind.

"What?" Kojo asked.

"I thought you said I was paranoid." She pursed her lips.

"Tell me anyway."

"Fine. I think the second car might be from the Doona shithead."

Kojo flinched and glanced at her. "You think he's following us. Why"

"Not him. Just someone he sent to track you. Because it's the kind of thing, the pile of dung would do. He runs the Wanai Secret Police, for goodness' sake. Putting surveillance on people is what he does."

"But I'm not Wanaian. I don't fall under his jurisdiction."

"Don't be naïve. He doesn't care. Plus, you lost his fiancée. He's not going to let you get away with it. He will punish you hard, so you should watch your back."

"Well, I think you should be the one watching your back since you're the one who abducted the princess."

"Make no mistake. I'm doing that already. Although, we'll be better if I watched your back and you watched mine."

He barked unamused laughter. "You think I'm going to trust you? Not happening."

"I'm not inclined to trust you either. But I believe we have one common enemy, Kweku Doona. Since we are stuck together for the duration of this journey. I propose that we call a truce until we get rid of the Doona spy. Afterwards, we can go back to pistols at dawn. What do you say?"

"I'll think about it."

"Fair enough. But think fast."

Finally, the car slowed as they hit traffic leading to the border town of Seme Krake. By the time they drove through the checkpoint, the sun was low in the sky.

"We should find somewhere to spend the night," she said.

"It's less than an hour to Cotonou. We'll find a hotel when we get there."

Chapter 9

Hours later, they arrived in Cotonou, the commercial centre of Benin Republic. It was a large coastal city with one of the busiest ports in the West African region.

Kojo drove through Boulevard St Michel, past the vast Dantokpa market, towards the city hotel he'd booked on his phone earlier. During the day, the market bustled with activities. Traders from neighbouring countries like Nigeria, Togo and Ghana came here to purchase items, mostly imported goods, to resell in their home countries. The ECOWAS treaty allowed for freedom of trade between member states.

Kojo was exhausted. Considering what had happened in the past forty-eight hours, it was no wonder.

Rain lashed the windscreen, the wipers swishing rapidly to clear the view. His brain took longer than usual to translate the French road signs, although he could speak the language a little. But the slow evening traffic helped, for a change, because he had more time to work out where he was going while they moved slowly.

The Satnav was on, but he knew that thing could be unreliable. He'd heard anecdotes of people directed into no-entry streets or the totally wrong place. He had to be vigilant since he was in unfamiliar territory. If only his brain didn't feel like it would shut down soon.

"If you tell me where we're going, I can help," Latifah's soft voice cut through his mind.

Heat pulsed through Kojo. He stiffened, hand curling around the steering wheel. "The same way you helped me last night?"

She crossed arms over her chest. "I thought we agree to call a truce. You can't keep bringing up what happened."

He jerked to glance at her. "The only reason we're in this car now is because of what you did. So, yes. I'll keep bringing it up."

She huffed in seeming exasperation. "Suit yourself."

"I will," he gritted out.

Traffic opened, and he accelerated, intending to enter the forecourt of a service station before he sported the well-known hotel's neon sign. He drove through the entrance instead, found a space and parked the car.

"We'll spend the night here," he said before pushing the door and stepping out. Flicking the button to unlock it, he strode to the boot and opened it. He lifted his leather travel bag and suit carrier.

Latifah joined him and took her carry-on luggage.

Kojo locked the car, and they strode through the palm-tree lined and ground-level spot-lit walkway. Inside, the foyer was bright lights and sleek surfaces. Low Afro-jazz music came from the bar lounge he could see through the entrance to his left. The hotel boasted a swimming pool area overlooking the beach. Shame he wouldn't be using the facilities.

"Bienvenue, madame et monsieur. Comment puis-je vous aider ?" The male receptionist in a white shirt and black tie greeted.

"Bonsoir. On a réservé au nom du Mr et Mrs Hamadou," Kojo replied, pulling out his phone for the reservation details.

"Bien sur. Un instant, s'il vous plait." He typed on the keyboard, checking the booking.

Meanwhile, Latifah said nothing. He wasn't sure if she understood French well enough to know that he'd booked the room for them as man and wife. He'd done so to avoid scrutiny.

This was Africa. A man and a woman sharing the same hotel room as a married couple would receive less attention than a couple checked in under different names.

Standing there quietly, gaze averted, Latifah looked the most docile he'd seen her. Anyone would think she was the compliant wife waiting for her husband to take care of their hotel check-in.

How deceptive. He knew better.

Instead, she was a criminal and a caught fugitive he was escorting across international borders so he could free the victim she'd abducted with her accomplices.

The man behind the counter confirmed their reservations and checked them in. Minutes later, they were in the lift going to the third floor. He faced the doors, one bag over his shoulders, the other in his other arm. Latifah stood next to him, her case in front of her.

Kojo stifled a yawn. He needed rest. But navigating sleep when he had a dangerous companion was going to prove tricky.

Luke had followed them in a different car and had a pre-booked room in this hotel too. So, he could watch Latifah while Kojo slept. But she wasn't anyone else's responsibility but Kojo's. Anyway, he couldn't risk her getting away again.

Outside the elevator, he walked to the door bearing the number on the cardholder and slid the key in the lock. It popped open.

He stood aside and waved for Latifah to go inside.

"Aren't you going to carry me over the threshold? We are husband and wife, remember?" she said in a teasing sultry voice that did something to his belly, which only annoyed him.

She understood French well enough to decipher the conversation with the hotel receptionist. He made a mental note for next time.

"If you were my wife and we were at home. Yes. But hotel rooms are for mistresses and fuck buddies," he bit out in contempt before he realised what he'd just said.

Before he could feel guilty about the vulgar words, she had a comeback.

"When you put it like that, who want to endure snores and 'not tonight' excuses when I can get head, great dick and still go home to sleep in peace and quiet," She spoke as she sashayed inside, dragging her carry-on case.

He rolled his eyes heavenwards, shaking his head before he followed her and shut the door. He flicked the latch to engage the lock. If she opened the door, the click would alert him.

A separate sitting area was partitioned from the bedroom with a cream upholstered settee and two armchairs tucked under a square table. A large TV was braced against the wall, a small fridge beneath the mini-bar next to it. Dark drapes hung over the window, which overlooked the swimming pool and the sea. The other room had a double bed, a wardrobe and an ensuite bathroom.

Latifah walked around, checking the place out. She placed her case on the stand inside the wardrobe. "I'm hungry. Shall we check out the restaurant?"

Kojo dumped his bags on the bedroom carpet and let out a sigh. He didn't want to share a room with her. But he had to keep an eye on her. He picked the room service menu and passed it over. "Order some food."

He wanted to find out her good her spoken French was, although she understood it.

Sitting in the armchair, she grabbed the phone at the table and spoke rapid-fire French into the handset. Then, she ordered for two—grilled chicken, yam fries, bean cakes and lettuce salad. For drinks, she asked for water which suited him fine.

The fluency of the language on her tongue meant she could be from a variety of French-speaking nations in Africa. He would bet she was

West African, though. This still left countries like Mali, Cote d'Ivoire, Guinea, Wanai, Mauritania, Niger, Senegal, Togo, Burkina Faso, and their current location, Benin. There were still other close countries like Chad and Cameroon, which shared borders with Bagumi.

Her skin tone and facial structure made her a southern West African, ruling out Mali, Niger, Mauritania, and Burkina Faso.

When she put the phone down, he asked the question on his mind. "Which country are you from?"

She leaned into the chair, crossing her legs. "I'm African."

"Africa is not a country," he retorted, eyes narrowing. She was playing games as usual.

"I don't have a country. I'm a nomad." She lifted her right shoulder in a lazy shrug.

Lowering his body onto the settee, he watched her face, trying to find a tell. She was hard to read sometimes. "You mean like the Tuareg or Fulani. Which one?"

The Tuareg were a nomadic tribe living around the Sahara Desert in Niger, Mali, and Burkina Faso. They lived in matrilineal clans, and women had a high status in their culture. The men wore a veil instead of the women. They were known to be excellent astronomers because of the clear desert night skies.

The Fulani were another nomadic tribe found around western Africa, including Niger, Mali, Nigeria, and Cameroon, who live by herding cattle. They had the most extensive mobile pastoral community globally, and ninety-nine percent of them were Muslims.

"Actually, I have a bit of both in my blood," she replied, meeting his gaze.

This meant she was part-Tuareg, part-Fulani. He wondered which other tribe made up the rest.

The answer didn't help him, but it was better than nothing. At least she gave some information. He could pass it along to his brother when he checked in later.

"So, your French is not classroom taught. It's lived, conversational fluency."

"Yes. I told you I'm an adventurer. I interact with people who speak different languages. My Spanish is passable, and since the Chinese descended on African soil in droves, I've had to learn Mandarin too."

She grabbed the remote and flicked on the TV. "What about you? How many languages do you speak?"

"Didn't you read that in my dossier?" He got off the sofa, strode into the bedroom and grabbed his overnight bag, placing it on the counter in the wardrobe, so he had a direct view from the bathroom. He couldn't risk leaving it out of sight while he washed his hands.

She was the kind of person who invaded people's privacy. Therefore, she would have no qualms going through his personal items with his back turned. He didn't want her touching his things, as petty as that might be.

"Why are you so uptight?" she asked, standing on the other side of the open bathroom door.

His spine stiffened. "I'm not uptight."

"You so are. Why are you angry that I read your dossier?" she retorted, chin lifted, eyes blazing with a challenge.

Was she not afraid of him? Did she think he was such a pushover? Someone she could taunt and ridicule.

Not in the mood for her nonsense games, he stepped into her personal space and grabbed her face in his palm.

Her skin was supple, smooth. She'd removed the glasses before she ate. He would bet they weren't prescriptions, just part of her disguise. Still, her brown eyes sparkled with fire.

He shouldn't let her goad him. He should be the bigger man, the gentleman.

Instead, he squeezed hard but not enough to cause damage.

Her eyes widened, and she gasped.

Her reaction sent a thrill down his spine, and his dick pulsed to life. He shoved down the unwelcome sensation. He could play too. "I'm angry because you invaded my privacy. You didn't have my permission to read the information."

This close to her, he caught a faint hint of perfume and her feminine musk. The urge to bury himself inside her was still there. But he wasn't going to let it rise to the surface.

He wasn't about to take the enemy into his bed.

She narrowed her eyes. "Have you never run a background check on the people visiting the palace. What? It's okay for you to invade people's privacy because you work for a king but not for us mere mortals to research your info."

He caught her insult about him working for royalty, but he didn't let it get to him. Instead, he tightened his grip a little. "Those people who visit the personal quarters of the palace give their consent for their backgrounds to be checked. It's the price for visiting the palace. I never gave you consent to check my background."

"So what? It's not the end of the world. Deal with it." She didn't even flinch, staring at him with that daring expression. There was no remorse for what she'd done. Not one iota.

He lowered his hand, gripped her neck, and slammed her back against the wall. A part of his wanted her to fight back like she'd done when he'd found her earlier today. But she didn't. It was almost as if she was offering her neck to him. As if she was getting some sort of thrill from his aggression.

Desire pulsed through him. The woman ruined his life. Yet he was so close to throwing caution to the wind and going twenty-toes with her against the wall of all things.

"Uh." He grunted in disgust and released her. He was suddenly tired, and the last place he wanted to be was anywhere near her. But until he found Princess Isha, he knew rest was a long way off.

A knock on the door saved him from doing anything else.

Latifah slipped under him and entered the bathroom. The panel clicked shut behind him.

"Who is it?" he asked, glad to escape the woman who had gotten under his skin since yesterday, if only temporarily. He walked out of the bedroom.

"Room service." The muffled voice came through, and he pulled the door open.

Two bellboys stood with covered dishes on silver trays. "Bonsoir, monsieur. Vous avez demandé le service d'étage ?"

"Oui. Come in." He moved aside as they entered, pulling his wallet from his back pocket.

He slipped out two 1000 West African CFA Francs banknotes. He'd been to the Bureau de Change after they'd crossed into the Benin Republic. The currency was legal tender in the French-speaking West African countries. Two of those countries were en route to Ghana from Nigeria. So, it made sense to get some cash.

After handing the cash to the men as they left, he locked the door again and waited for Latifah to come of the bathroom.

Not saying a word to him, she went straight to the table, opened the coverings, and took some plates to the coffee table. Then she settled on the settee and ate while watching the TV.

He moved the armchair, so he didn't have his back to her and sat in it. Then he ate his meal. It tasted good, although his state of mind didn't allow him to appreciate anything special about it. Nevertheless, it was the first proper meal he'd had all day aside from the cupcake Princess Amara had offered this afternoon.

They ate in silence. Well, the TV, set on the news channel, provided background noise. Afterwards, he cleared the dishes away and put the tray outside the room for the staff to pick up.

He tugged a bunch of zip ties from his jacket pocket and went inside, keeping the hand hidden from Latifah's line of sight. He had to maintain the element of surprise. "Do you want to use the shower tonight?"

"Why?" she asked in a nonchalant voice.

"It's a yes or no answer."

"Then, no."

"Sit in the armchair."

"Why?"

He didn't reply. He walked up to her, scooped her out of the settee and dumped her into the armchair.

"Ooh. Is this some kind of primitive mating ritual?" She stretched out her arm towards his face.

He took advantage, gripped her wrist, and lowered it to the armrest, at the same time looping and knotting a tie into place.

She looked down and jerked upright. "What the hell are you doing?"

He gripped the other arm, but she struggled this time, lashing out. He used his body weight like in a rugby tackle and held her in place, ensuring she couldn't move her legs. He hadn't forgotten how she'd kicked him in the groin earlier.

He restrained her other arm and went to work on her legs. This was trickier, and he had to keep his head and body out of range of her kicks as she struggled and cursed him.

By the time he was done, they were both breathing heavily and sweating.

After a while, she dragged in slow inhalations and exhalations and cocked her head to look at him as he straightened. Her fists clenched, and her jaw tightened. Her spine and shoulders stayed rigid. Her chin was tilted in a proud and stubborn angle.

"Why am I tied up?" she asked in a calm voice, looking up at him with big brown eyes filled with defiance and something else he couldn't decipher immediately.

Whatever it was, he couldn't forget who she was. She was the enemy, the one who had stolen Princess Isha. God only knew what was happening to the royal right now.

He'd never bound a woman like this. Never restrained one against her wishes like he'd just done to this one.

But Latifah wasn't innocent. She was a criminal. The only reason she wasn't in prison right now was because he hadn't found Isha.

So, he shouldn't care if Latifah was uncomfortable. Still, he carried her and the chair into the bedroom and set it close to the window, facing the TV. He was still considerate. He really needed to scrub away the lifetime habits of a gentleman.

He sat on the bed and took his boots and socks off. He placed them on the other side of the bed, away from her. Then he took his jacket off and hung it in the wardrobe.

She just watched him, probably waiting for him to explain his actions.

"I need a shower, and I want you still in this room when I get out," he turned and headed towards the bathroom.

"You don't need to tie me up. I promised I would take you to the princess," she sounded frustrated.

"I don't trust you." He took his bag into the bathroom and shut the door. He took his shoulder holster off and placed it on the counter. Then he took his kit out and shaved first. He didn't think he'd have time in the morning to do it.

Afterwards, he stripped and stepped into the shower, glad for the needle pricks of lukewarm water on his skin. Sighing, he grabbed the soap and washed his skin.

Ten minutes later, he was out and pulling on a t-shirt and pair of shorts. He grabbed his bag, opened the door, and returned to the room. Leaving the pack in the wardrobe, he hung up his trousers and shirt.

Then he padded to the other side of the bed, placed his weapon in the bedside drawer and climbed in, settling on his back, and pulling the sheet over him. He switched off the light as well as the TV. Darkness descended, only broken by light through the edges of the curtain.

"You can untie me now," she said in a calm tone, her voice filling the room.

"No," he replied in a matching voice.

"You're going to leave me in the chair all night?"

"Yes."

"That's cruel."

"Cruel?" He jerked upright, switching the bedside lamp on. "Cruel is you abducting another human being and putting her friends and family through worry and anguish."

Her breath hitched, and her pupils dilated. After a while, she closed her eyes and puffed out a heavy breath. "Fine. I was cruel."

"You are still cruel by not telling me where she is. By not releasing her."

"I'm not trying to be cruel. I'm trying to save people's lives."

"Ha. That's rich."

"You won't understand."

"Maybe not. We'll never know because you still refuse to tell me."

Her fingers wrapped around the armrests in a white-knuckle grip. Still, she said nothing.

After a few seconds of silence, he lay back down and switched off the light.

Sleep didn't come easily. For the second night in a row, he was restless.

He lay still, ears straining for sound, listening for any movement or whimpers from her. Only silence greeted him. His emotions wavered from disappointment to anger to sympathy. Ever since he'd met Latifah, his feelings had been all over the place. But he refused to let them out again. He would not be made a fool again.

He needed to hold onto the rage, though.

To hell with this. Huffing, he rolled out of bed and padded to the minibar and reached for a bottle of whisky. He unscrewed the cap, tossed his head back and gulped down the liquid until it emptied.

He only caught the hint of vanilla and oak flavours when most of it was gone and the liquor burned through his belly. Still wired, he took a second bottle, brandy this time, and did the same. It was probably not a good idea to mix the alcohol, but he didn't care.

While Latifah was restrained, he needed to catch some sleep, not spend the night thinking about her.

Tossing the bottles into the bin, he returned and climbed into bed. Minutes later, the alcohol in his veins had the desired effect and he drifted to sleep.

"Kojo."

The soft sound of his name made him jerk awake, reaching for his weapon as he flicked the switch. A dim light filled the room.

Latifah sat in the chair, still bound. "I need to use the toilet."

He puffed out air and looked at his wristwatch. He'd slept for about two hours. It would probably have to do.

Sighing, he padded out of bed, reached in his jacket for his flip knife and walked over to slice the bindings off. He leaned back when he finished.

She stood, grabbed stuff from her bag and walked into the bathroom.

He returned to sit on the bed, waiting for her.

She took longer than he thought. Then he heard the running water of the shower.

He shifted and turned the TV back on, flicking until he found a movie channel.

He lay there, half-listening to the bathroom and half-drifting.

When she came out, she wore a pair of white cotton shorts and a T-shirt, the hair wrapped in a bun. She walked over to the armchair and sat back in it. She shifted around, seemingly trying to get comfortable. In the end, she pulled her legs up, tucked them into the corner and rested her head on her arms.

She appeared tiny and different from the woman who had faced him down. She looked vulnerable.

His chest constricted, getting heavier and difficult to breathe the longer he watched her.

He lay back down and turned off the light. Yet, he remained unsettled.

He couldn't do this. Couldn't let her sleep in the chair, and he didn't want to bind her again.

"Come to the bed," he said in a quiet voice.

She didn't reply, and there was no sound of movement.

He flicked on the light.

She stared at him, blinking.

"Did you hear me?" He raised a brow.

"Yes. But I wanted to be sure I heard you right. You're inviting me to sleep on the bed?"

"Yes."

She uncurled her body and walked tentatively over. Tugging the corner of the sheet out, she climbed in.

She lay on her side, facing him. "Why?"

"It doesn't matter. Just sleep."

He probably wasn't going to sleep properly again anyway since he had to be alert. He switched off the light and lay on his back staring up at the ceiling.

"Thank you." She sighed. "For what it's worth. I will take you to see the princess, even if I don't do or say anything else. That's a promise."

He didn't reply. He had nothing to say except he would only believe it when he saw it. He wasn't about to drop another guard for her.

After a few minutes, he heard the steady pattern of her breathing as she fell asleep.

He woke to soft, warm, feminine curves plastered to his chest and his arm draped around her body.

Latifah.

How did he get into this position? He must have dozed off at some point.

He tried to jerk away, but she held onto his arm. "Please, don't go."

For some reason, he didn't fight her. Maybe it was the way she pleaded. Maybe his mind was still hazy from a dream, or it was the alcohol he'd drunk earlier. Whatever.

When she tugged his right hand under her t-shirt and onto her breast, he didn't pull back. Instead, his breath stuck in his lungs in anticipation.

Her breast perfectly fit his hand, and he gently coaxed the nipple into a stiff point.

She whimpered and dragged his other hand into her shorts, placing it over her mound.

He didn't do anything, though, just rested it there. He was walking a tight wire, knowing he shouldn't be doing this, shouldn't be touching her. She was still the enemy.

Yet, his body was wound tight. His dick hardening by the second. He didn't take his hands away.

What was he doing?

What was she doing to him? How was she making him crave her even after everything? When was the last time he'd had a woman in his arms? He couldn't remember.

Before he could think better of it, he dropped an open-mouthed kiss where her neck met her shoulder and dragged his lips against the sensitive flesh. He nipped the skin with his teeth.

Her body shuddered against his.

"Please, more," she whispered.

He ignored her plea, determined to go at his own pace. Instead, he tweaked her breast, moulding and tugging.

She moaned, pushing her boob into his palm.

Approval was like liquid heat in his veins. He rewarded her by grazing his teeth against her shoulder, making her shiver again.

His dick was aching now and digging into her backside.

"Take your shorts off," he said.

She didn't hesitate, pushing it down and wiggling until she tossed it onto the floor. She tried to lie on her back, but he held her in place, not wanting to change her position. Not wanting to look directly in her face.

Perhaps if he didn't see her face, he wouldn't have to acknowledge whom he was lusting after. He wouldn't have to admit that he was in bed with the enemy. Someone who had hurt the people he cared about. The woman who had ruined his life. Someone he should hate.

Yet the thing coursing through his veins and heating his blood wasn't hatred.

He pulled his dick out, positioned it against her bum cheeks and thrust forward. It slipped between her thighs. He groaned at the feel of her heat and skin. He was steel, and she was velvet.

He rolled his pelvis again. His dick glided along her pussy, and she coated him in wetness and juices.

She moaned again, her body clenching around him.

His dick was just between her thighs, rubbing along her pussy, yet it felt like he was touching bliss. All he needed to do was lift her leg, change the angle of his thrust and he would slide deep inside her. But he fought the urge. There were some lines he wasn't ready to cross. Not yet.

She tugged his hand, trying to get it to her core, but he just hovered above it, leaving ghost touches and not engaging her labia.

Her breathing was choppy, and her body wound tight.

"Touch me," she said in a husky whisper. She held her breath, her stomach clenching.

"Tell me something first, and I'll give you what you want." He knew he was falling to new lows by using sex as a tool to get what he wanted too. She'd used it against him before. And he was in bed with the last person on earth he should touch. So, he'd already fallen from grace and was heading to Hell. He might as well make sure it was worth the ride.

"What do you want to know?" her voice was breathy.

He kept pumping his hips, hitting her clit with each go. But it wasn't enough to give her completion.

"Tell me why you hate Kweku Doona so much?" he whispered in a gruff voice.

She froze, and he pinched her nipple, making her squirm.

"Unfair," she protested.

"Tell me." He twisted the nipple again.

She arched into him, moaning. "There are so many reasons why I hate him."

"Then tell me the one reason that is personal to you." He pumped his hips again.

"The bastard nearly killed my aunt when he threw her off a balcony. As it is, her life is permanently changed." Her words were tainted with anguish and hurt.

Shit. He stiffened, tried to move back.

She gripped his hand. "Don't you dare stop. I don't want to talk about it. I gave you what you wanted. Now, give me what I need."

When she lowered his hand onto her pussy, he obliged her and slid his fingers through and around the slick flesh. He flicked, teased, caressed the sensitive flesh, going up and down in circular motions. At the same time, he kept rocking his hips, his dick sliding against her pussy.

He forgot all else, focused on the jolts of arousal piercing through him even as he played her body, her breast, her nipple, her clit.

She writhed and moaned. It all got too much. Lost in a frenzy, he gripped her nape, turned her head so he could claim her mouth in a fierce kiss that shook even him. Her mouth was soft and full and perfect. Their tongues tangled, dipping in and out, twirling around each other.

His fingers played her body, and he sensed the slight tremors in her body, building with tension as she chased the orgasm. Soon she was shuddering and arching and gasping into his mouth and pushing her ass against his dick even harder.

He kissed her until the energy dissipated from her body, then he pulled away and lay on his back, tucking his unspent hard dick back into his shorts. He wouldn't be satisfied until he knew the princess was safe and well.

That thought washed his arousal away and deflated his dick.

Chapter 10

Hours later, Latifah was still trying to get her head around what had happened last night between her and Kojo.

She stared at the scenery whizzing past the highway, the sun high in the sky.

They had left Cotonou before dawn and traversed the border into Togo. Staying on the coastal route to Lomé, from where they crossed another border into Ghana. Now they were driving to Accra, which was still another two hours away. Kojo's diplomatic pass meant navigating through international boundaries were hassle-free. Also, the countries were all part of the ECOWAS agreement, which allowed free travel between participating nations.

She glanced at Kojo.

He stared straight ahead as if he was avoiding looking at her. He hadn't said much since their sexy encounter in bed.

Yesterday had been a mixed bag of a day.

Starting with her irritation that Kojo had caught her. Then trying to hold back rage when she'd seen Kweku in the hotel swimming and had to fight the urge to jump into the water and slit his throat. Afterwards came the remorse when she'd seen Princess Amara's heartbreak.

Then she'd vowed she would take Kojo to Wanai, and the start of the road trip had culminated in their night in the Cotonou hotel.

Kojo was a man of multiple layers, to her surprise.

He was a man dedicated to this job and to his family. Dubbed gentle giant. While his brawny size could be intimidating and served as a protective barrier for those in his care, he wasn't known to be rough or unkind.

Imagine her shock when Kojo had tied her to the chair. She hadn't seen that coming. Never knew he was capable of being harsh, especially to a woman.

From everything she'd read about him, including her previous encounters with him, he wasn't violent or prone to losing his temper. He wasn't even aggressive.

Usually, people saw his size and backed away, so there were no reports of him being in any brawls. The only place he showed any kind of aggression was on the rugby field. But that was within the rules of the game, which he loved so much.

He wasn't even kinky sexually. His response to her taunts about sex had proven him to be as vanilla as the guy next door.

But when they'd argued just outside the hotel bathroom, and he'd shoved her against the wall. She'd seen it then.

The caged rage simmering beneath the surface. And something else he tethered—desire, hot smoking desire.

He withheld those things by choice.

It wasn't that he couldn't be violent. It was that he chose not to be. He was a man comfortable in his own skin. He didn't have to prove anything to anyone.

Then he'd shocked her by binding her to the chair. No matter how she'd fought him, he'd used his size against her.

She'd tried to soften him up for batting her long lashes and playing nice. It hadn't worked.

Instead, he'd showered, changed, and gotten into bed. Then he'd left her on the chair and fallen asleep.

To be fair, she'd deserved it and worse.

If he'd handed her over to Kweku, sleeping in a chair would have been the least of her worries. The bastard would have her tortured at the very least.

The memory of what the horrible man had done to her cousin returned, making bile rise to her throat.

She shook off the feeling and remembered something else. "I have to check in again."

"You can do so when we reach Accra," Kojo replied without looking at her.

She didn't argue. There was no point. She was still within the window to call home and let them know she was safe.

Her mind drifted back to last night when Kojo allowed her to get into bed. She'd fallen asleep next to him only to wake later while he'd slept. Without much thought, she'd shifted close to him, welcoming his warmth as he'd cocooned her.

Then he'd woken and tried to pull away, but she'd begged him to stay. He'd felt good, and she'd yearned for more. Longed to forget the circumstances of their meeting or why they'd been in the hotel room together and just enjoy each other, if only briefly.

He'd obliged, and she'd taken it a step further. Soon they'd been writhing against each other, and he'd taken her to bliss.

Yet, he'd withheld his own pleasure and hadn't climaxed.

It was as if he was determined not to take pleasure from her. As if she was something tainted.

It had hurt. Still, she understood.

He didn't trust her.

Nevertheless, it showed he was a decent human being. He could have shoved her onto the floor when she'd touched him. He could have rejected her outright. Especially after she'd answered the question he'd asked. He didn't have to follow through or keep his promise.

She puffed out a heavy breath.

It was up to her to gain his trust. The only way he would believe her was when he saw the princess for himself. Hopefully, in a few hours, they would be in Wanai and close to their destination.

Kojo pulled the car into a service station car park. There were restaurants and shops as well as a petrol station.

He got out, and she followed him. A teenage girl sat under an umbrella advertising phone service.

"Can I make the call now?" Latifah asked, pointing at the phone girl.

"Go ahead." He waited while she walked up to the vendor.

"I need to use your phone," Latifah said.

The girl greeted her and quoted the price per minute.

Latifah agreed and took the phone. She dialled her answering service, listened to the message:

Counsel has agreed to help us. Going to show her the sights. Won't be here when you arrive. Back in a few days.

Positive news. Zain seemed to have convinced Princess Isha—counsel—to help them raise awareness for devastating ethnic cleansing going on in Wanai. It was only the start but a significant step. Only time would tell if the outcome would justify their actions.

Latifah cut off the call and asked the phone girl. "How much for data? I want to check my email quickly."

The girl eyed her as she mentioned an amount.

Latifah pulled out cash from her wallet and gave her more than necessary. Opened an incognito browser on the smartphone, logged onto an encrypted server and then a messaging service where she sent a short message. *Home soon.*

She cleared the cache and deleted the number she'd called for the answering service. Then she handed the phone back to the girl.

"Madam, your change." The girl tried to hand her some notes.

"Keep it." Latifah pulled out more notes and gave them to her. "And this is for forgetting my face if anyone asks."

The girl shrugged. "I don't know you."

"Good." Latifah headed back towards Kojo.

Interesting that he'd waited by the car instead of shadowing her.

"Is everything okay?" he asked, searching her face.

"Yes. The princess is well, and they are still expecting us."

"Okay. Let's get something to eat." He strode to the fast-food restaurant busy with midday diners and glanced around.

"Do you want to use the ladies?" He wasn't looking at her.

"Not at the moment," she replied, following his gaze, and pretending she wasn't curious about what he was doing.

"Order something to eat and find a table over this end. I need to talk to someone," he said.

"Okay." She joined the queue for the counter while watching him.

He waved at someone before walking towards a man seated at a four-seat table. The man kept a curious gaze on her as Kojo approached. The two of them hugged and settled in the chairs.

They were about ten to twelve meters away, so she couldn't hear their conversation. But, at one point, both glanced in her direction.

Latifah recognised the man with Kojo. He was Razi Hamadou, Kojo's brother who worked for the Bagumi Intelligence Service. Razi had worked with Latifah on a mission years ago.

This was going to be an exciting encounter.

Actually, it was terrible. Since Razi was here, it meant the BIS knew her identity.

Latifah's heart raced, and adrenaline rushed through, setting her in a fight or flight mode. She glanced around the place, looking for how to get away.

Were there other agents here to apprehend her? Was Kojo going to hand her over to the authorities? He'd promised he would let her go if she cooperated, which she'd done so far. So, what changed?

If his intention was to hand her over, it was foolish of him to let her stand by herself. Unless, of course, there were others just waiting for her to run so they could apprehend her.

Her gaze bounced around the place, looking at people's faces, trying to pick up actions that seemed out of the ordinary, looking for faces she may have seen recently.

She'd sworn they'd been followed from Nigeria, anyway. But since they left Cotonou, she hadn't noticed any trailing vehicles.

She glanced around again. Two men stood outside the restaurant. They just stood there, not doing anything else. Were they part of Razi Hamadou's team?

She glanced back at Kojo, who was looking at her with a frown on his face.

Shit.

She sucked in a deep breath, needing to keep calm. If she ran, then their deal was off. She would figure out why his brother was here and face up to it. She could only hope the honourable Kojo would stick up for her.

"Madam, what would you like?" the woman at the counter asked, drawing her attention away from her unease.

She ordered food, waited for it to be served and took it towards the table.

Kojo stood as she approached. "Razi, this is Latifah."

His brother outstretched his hand, still seated. "Nice to see you, Ms Kamto."

"Likewise, Mr Hamadou." His handshake was firm and brief.

Latifah pulled out a seat and parked her bum opposite Razi and next to Kojo.

Kojo glanced from her to his brother. "Do you know each other?"

"I suppose you should know," Razi spoke up. "Ms Kamto was a freelancer contracted with the BIS. She did a job for us a few years ago, and we occasionally use her as a consultant."

"What?" Kojo's gaze bounced between the two of them, and he raised his hands in defeat. "You know what? Just keep an eye on her. I need to use the gents."

Then he walked off.

"Your brother is wound tighter than a Grandfather Clock," she commented as she watched his hulking body glide across the aisles of the busy fast-food restaurant.

"I can understand why this time." Razi followed her gaze before turning to scrutinise her. "So, Black Widow, why did you abduct a member of the Bagumian royal family?"

Unease wormed through Latifah's gut at the use of her code name. Sitting face to face with someone who knew her alias meant her cover was blown, and the end was near for her. Prison looked like a likely path for her future if she wasn't assassinated first. Perhaps she should have run when she had the chance.

"Are you wired?" she asked, holding his gaze.

He laughed. "No."

"I don't believe you. Come with me." She stood, and he followed her into the corridor leading to the toilets.

She shoved him against the wall.

"Easy, Ms Kamto." Razi raised her hands in a conciliatory gesture.

She didn't buy his easy surrender. Shaking her head, she leaned in and patted down his body, checking that he wasn't wearing a wire.

He was athletic and as tall as Kojo. But not as broad, and Kojo outmuscled him. There were similarities, making it apparent they were brothers, like the skin tone and wide nose. But he wasn't Kojo. Kojo was the one she wanted in and out of bed.

Satisfied, she stepped back a little. She didn't find anything obvious, not even a weapon.

"Why are you here?" she whispered, leaning in, so others would not overhear.

"You abducted a member of the Bagumian royal family," he said in an equally low voice.

"You know I cannot confirm that statement. However, I can tell you that my sources say that the royal is in safe hands and will be home soon."

"Intact?"

"Absolutely. No damage. As far as anyone is concerned, she's on an incognito break, that's all."

"How long?"

"About a week."

"Right. We'll give you the time. Only because I know what this is about, and you have done some good work for Bagumi. We know about her past relationship with the professor. But you better make sure she gets home in one piece, or you know there's nowhere on earth you can hide. I won't be able to help you."

"I know. Thank you." She breathed a sigh of relief as they returned to the restaurant.

Razi hadn't come to apprehend her. Not yet. Her colleagues were not in danger. Perhaps they would achieve their aims. *If Almighty wills it.*

Kojo sat at the table. "Meet me in the car when you finish eating."

He got up abruptly and walked out without giving her a second glance.

"I'll see you around," Razi said and followed his brother.

Something was wrong with the way Kojo had stormed out. Also, he'd never left her alone before, so it was strange that he was leaving her alone now.

She ate quickly, hurried outside and across the forecourt towards the parked car. Kojo was already in the driver's seat when she got in.

He didn't say anything but kept clenching his hands around the steering wheel and releasing it.

Something had gone wrong. She'd never seen him this agitated, this unsettled, even when they'd argued.

She worked saliva into her dry mouth. "What's going on?"

His grip was white-knuckled. A pulse thumped on his temple. "Did you fuck my brother?"

The question was so random, so out of the blue, she was momentarily gobsmacked. "What?"

He twisted in his seat and met her gaze. There was something in his eyes. Cold. Ruthless. She'd never seen him like this before. Not even when he'd captured her at the safehouse.

"I'll ask you again. Do you fuck my brother?" his voice was calm and icy.

A shiver went down her spine. "Kojo, where is this coming from?"

He closed his eyes, exhaled noisily, and lifted his dark lashes. "I'm not going to play your game. Not today. Not anymore." He raised his hand and pointed out of the windshield. "You see that SUV over there. It's full of BIS agents. All I have to do is indicate, and they will come here and take you away."

She looked out, saw a man standing beside the car he indicated. It was one of the men she'd seen outside the restaurant. She'd been right. The BIS agents were here for her. But what about the reassurance from Razi?

Shit.

Her stomach rolled, her chest tingles with dread as her palms got clammy.

"I'm going to ask you one last time. Did. You. Fuck my brother," his voice stayed low, the rumble full of threat.

"No," she said with resignation.

He didn't reply immediately, and her heart raced. Did he believe her? What was he going to do? The tingling in her chest increased, and she swallowed with difficulty.

She'd never cared before if he believed her. Yet, now she wanted his trust more than ever.

"About Princess Isha," he spoke finally. "Swear to me that aside from the way you took her, she will not come to any harm."

She clutched a palm to her chest. "I swear it. She is unharmed."

He stayed quiet for a few more seconds, then straightened and clipped his harness on. "Put your seatbelt on."

She did, still eyeing him and wondering what he was up to. It was frustrating to be on the defensive, not knowing what he would do. But she just had to suck it up. She would rather put up with the unpredictable Kojo than deal with BIS agents.

He started the engine, reversed, and drove out to the main road.

But they didn't go far.

He pulled into the entrance of a hotel and found a space to park.

"I'm going to book a room for the night," he said, the engine still running. "I'm too wired to drive this evening. So, we'll head out of Accra tomorrow."

They'd been on the road for over ten hours, and they'd crossed two borders. But there was still a couple of hours before dusk.

"You know I can drive," she commented. She'd thought he was in a hurry to get to the princess. Although according to the message she'd received earlier, the princess wouldn't be there when they arrived.

Still, he didn't know it. So, she probably should tell him. But he was acting weird.

She would wait to find out what was going on.

"I know," he replied in a heavy tone. "But you're not insured to drive this car. If anything happens ...."

This was the Kojo she knew, a stickler for the rules.

She didn't argue. "Okay."

He stared out of the window. "We don't have to share the same room. The BIS agents will stay with you."

That hit her like a punch in the gut. Her chest tightened, making it difficult to breathe. She hadn't thought it would hurt this much to be rejected by him. Had last night been so awful for him? Her throat clogged up, and she swallowed several times. "Separate rooms? Why? If this is about last night, I promise—"

"If we share the same room, I'm going to fuck you." He cut her off. Desire burned bright in his intense gaze, visible to see.

Damn. Her core clenched. Her breath hitched, her pulse racing.

He wasn't rejecting her. Instead, he was laying his cards on the table. He wouldn't be able to resist her again if they were in the same confined space. He was letting her make a choice to be with him or not.

Warmth flooded her body and her mouth moistened. She craved him. The urge to touch him made her fingers itch. Wanted him so very much. More than she wished for anyone else or anything right now.

"Yes," she breathed. "I want that. I want you."

He nodded once and killed the engine. Then he reached in his jacket pocket and pulled out a folded card which he passed to her. It was his medical card. On the inside was listed his blood type—O+, sickle cell genotype—AA, organ donation consent— yes, HIV status—negative, date of last HIV test— January 2018.

That was two months ago.

"I haven't had any sexual encounter for months. Neither have I had any blood transfusions. So, I'm clean," Kojo said as if it was the most natural thing to talk about. He had no qualms laying himself bare for her. Although he'd been furious yesterday because she'd read his dossier. The difference here? He gave her the information voluntarily. "What is your HIV status?"

Okay. That was direct but expected since he'd just revealed his medical history to her.

She handed the card back to him. "I'm clean. My last test was in February."

"And when was the last time you fucked anyone?" His gaze didn't waver.

The questions pissed her off, considering she just told him she was clean. It seemed not enough for him.

"It's none of your business," she retorted.

"It is my business if you want me to eat your pussy." He didn't even flinch.

Her insides contracted, and her pulse rate skyrocketed.

Damn, he knew how to drive a hard bargain. She definitely wanted his mouth on her core, sucking her clit.

"Fine," she said in a breathy voice. "It's been months. Six months almost since I had a lover."

His eyes sparkled, and his lips tugged up at the corner in a satisfied smile.

Then he opened the door and stepped out. He walked to the boot and opened it.

She joined him there and grabbed her bag. Side by side, they walked to the hotel entrance, entered the lobby.

"Good afternoon, sir. How can I help you?" The receptionist greeted.

"We would like a room for the night."

"Sure. We have a room. I'll get you checked in." She slid a sheet of paper to him. "Please fill this in."

He completed the form, signing them in as Mr and Mrs Hamadou, the same as in Cotonou. He'd said Africans were less judgemental about a man and a woman sharing a room if they were man and wife. Plus, he didn't want to draw attention to them anyway.

She appreciated him trying to save her face and keep her secure in a way.

He picked up the keys, and they walked to the lifts. They stood perfectly still in the elevator, which had another man. Tension arced in the air.

Latifah's heart raced. She wanted to grab Kojo and kiss him. Wished to press him against the wall and touch him. Didn't care about the stranger in their midst.

But she cared about Kojo, and he wouldn't want any public displays.

They stepped out of the lift and turned left, walked a few metres to their room. He slid the key onto the lock, pushed the door and held it for her to enter.

As soon as the heavy door swung shut, he shoved her against the wall and grabbed her throat. Enough to keep her in place without choking.

Surprised, her breath bitched, her pulse beating fast against his palm.

Damn. Just watching him stand over her was exhilarating. She could flip the situation if she wanted. But she didn't. Instead, she tipped her head back, offering her neck, her surrender. She would play it his way for now.

"Hey, big guy." She stared up through hooded eyes, purring the last two words affectionately.

His eyes darkened, and his throat rippled. Yes, she could bring him to his knees. But she loved the way he pushed against her, rolling his groin against hers. He pinned her, parting her legs with his own.

She dug her fingers into his shoulders, gripping him as she raised her legs and wrapped them around his hips. Her skirt rode up her thighs, only her panties and the fabric of his trousers separating them.

"Are you still sure you want to do this?" His voice was husky. The hand on her throat curled around the back. His thumb stroked the bottom of her earlobe. His other hand gripped her butt, fingers digging into her crease.

It wasn't just lust between them. There was something else. Something she refused to acknowledge. She would focus on the sex. Only the sex.

"Yes," she cupped his face. "I want you buried deep inside me."

"Unh," he groaned before pressing his mouth hers in a fierce kiss.

She returned the kiss, opening and invading his mouth with her tongue. He tasted of spice and Kojo, and she wanted more. So much more of him.

Then his fingers were between her legs. He shoved her panties to one side and stroked her pussy.

She moaned into his mouth, pushing against his hand. Tingles skittered over her skin, intoxication flooding her blood.

Kojo fingered and teased her, making her squirm and writhe. He drove her insane.

She lowered her hand to his trousers, unbuckled his belt, undid the button and zip.

Pulling back, he stared at her with the darkened eyes, his breathing choppy. He reached in his back pocket and pulled out a packet of condoms. She wasn't sure when he put one in there. While he was waiting in the car, perhaps.

When he tore the foil, she took it. "Let me."

Shoving his boxers down, he freed his thick, solid erection and groaned as she rolled the condom onto him. It was as if he lost control as she rubbed his sheathed dick against her slick pussy and, with one shove, was lodged inside her.

"Oh."

"Unh"

They both gasped at the sensation. A twinge of pain making her stiffen. He was snug and taking him in all at once was almost impossible. Her breaths came in short, desperate snatches. She wanted more. She wanted all of him.

Kojo rammed deeper into her wet heat, and he groaned. "You are so warm and tight. Match parfait, cherie."

His husky words filled her with warmth, making her insides melt. The way he wielded dirty talk and endearments rattled the bricks she'd built around her heart.

And she didn't want to go there. She just wanted to enjoy this man for the little time she had him. Nothing else mattered as he started moving. Just the feel of his hardness, his heat, his strength. It felt so good.

"Tu me fais du bien, big guy." She whispered in French, telling him how good he made her feel.

Having him like this was a thrill. He was a different person, yet the same one she was attracted to when she'd first set eyes on him. There was something forbidden about what they were doing since they were technically adversaries.

But he yearned for her just like she craved him.

One hand holding her nape, the other gripping her hip, he nipped her ear lobe, her shoulder, her neck. Kojo kept thrusting, right there against the wall, rolling his hips and grazing her clit, making her writhe and moan and respond at the most basic level.

And the way he groaned with each ram inside her showed he loved it too.

She clawed, rocked, arousal melting her insides, making her tremble from the inside out.

Kojo reached down, fingers between their bodies and stroked her clit.

"Oh." Just the one-touch and Latifah tumbled into an orgasm, quivering and clenching around his length.

It seemed to pull him into one as well as he thrust harder and faster. Finally, his pleasure crested, and he bore down on her and emptied his seed inside her.

He leaned his sweaty forehead on hers as they both panted and tried to catch their breaths. His chest expanded and contracted, his muscles rippling and trembling. The sounds of their breathing, the smell of lust were in the air.

He carried her over to the bed and lay her down with him on top. He pressed a kiss into her before pulling out and going to the bathroom.

Latifah lay there, contentment rolling through her. They hadn't even taken their clothes off.

Chapter 11

Kojo wasn't thinking about the topsy-turvy situation his life had become when he walked out of the bathroom to see the lazy smile on Latifah's face. She lay flat on the bed of the impromptu hotel room he'd booked.

This morning when he'd climbed out of the hotel bed in Cotonou and got dressed, he'd been determined to forget his encounter with Latifah on that same bed last night. The taste of her need on his tongue as he'd kissed her. The way she'd felt in his arms as he'd brought her to climax.

He'd been annoyed at himself for succumbing to the temptation she presented when he'd woken and found himself wrapped around her luscious body.

The morning had gone well too. Before they'd left, he'd called his brother, who'd confirmed a rendezvous point in Accra. He'd been looking forward to seeing his brother and getting some direct expert opinion on his situation.

He'd also called Luke, checking in and getting an update.

Afterwards, Kojo and Latifah had packed up and left the hotel before dawn, heading west to Togo and crossing into Ghana. They'd driven in near silence, only interrupted by occasional talk radio and music. Latifah had seemed lost in her own thoughts.

Kojo had driven to the rendezvous point. Then, while Latifah went to the mobile phone stall, Kojo called Razi and confirmed his brother was already in the restaurant waiting.

He'd wanted time to talk to his brother privately, so he told Latifah to order her food. She joined the queue, and he strolled to Razi.

"Hey, *ti frè*." His brother greeted in their native Creole as he stood.

"*Mwen pi gran pase ou, frè.*" Grinning, Kojo shook his head as he embraced Razi. The irony of it was that Kojo was taller, heavier, and bigger than his siblings. Yet they still called him 'little brother'. His oldest brother was '*gran frè,*' meaning 'big brother'.

"Haven't you heard? Size doesn't matter." Razi grinned.

His middle brother was the family joker. Kojo shook his head slowly, although he couldn't help the upward tilt of his lips. "I'm not getting drawn into another of your dick jokes."

They settled in the chairs, and Razi said, "So, that's the *dam* giving you a hard time."

They both turned and glanced in Latifah's direction. She stood in the queue, looking at them.

"Yes, that's her. Did you find out anything about her?" he grabbed his brother's glass of coke and took a long sip.

"Yes. But I'm not sure you want to know," Razi replied.

"What do you mean?"

"Well, most of it is classified."

"Huh?" Kojo narrowed his eyes, and then it hit him. "She's a covert agent?"

Razi nodded.

Kojo glanced at Latifah again. No wonder. Her actions made sense. But how was she linked to the First Princess?

"Is she Bagumian?"

"No. She is Wanaian."

"Of course. No wonder she hates Kweku Doona. She said the man nearly killed her aunt."

"She told you that? Yes, Mrs Bassong. That was about ten years ago. Her son, Latifah's cousin, was in a relationship with the First Princess while she was in London."

"That was before I started working at the palace." Kojo tilted his head, thinking. "And now the same princess is engaged to Kweku. Do you think that's why she was taken?"

"Could be. I think she's with Professor Bassong and his siblings. We tracked the crew from the private jet that landed in Tambao. The descriptions are vague, but I think it was the Bassong team who took her, which means she could be in Wanai."

So Latifah was truthful. She was taking him to Wanai, to the princess. Kojo breathed a sigh of relief.

"I brought a crew to stay with you for the rest of the journey. Parts of Wanai are in a war zone, and if the princess is where I think she is, then you might need backup."

"No, that won't work. I promised Latifah we would make the journey just the two of us. She promised to take me to the princess."

"And you trust her?"

"Well, she's kept to the bargain so far." His mind flashed back to last night in the bed. Touching her intimately and listening to the sounds of her pleasure hadn't been part of the bargain.

At that point, Latifah turned up with a tray of food, and Kojo introduced the two. But it turned out both already knew each other well.

He used the opportunity to go to the gents. When he came out, he found Latifah and Razi making out in the corridor. Well, it looked like they were making out by the way her hands roamed Razi's body while she whispered in his ear.

Kojo's gut burned with jealousy. He'd never been jealous of anything until that very moment. The thought that his brother could be lovers with Latifah drained him of every other emotion.

It brought to clarity the notion he hadn't wanted to acknowledge. He wanted Latifah for himself. Regardless of what she'd done. Yet, she was a woman who passed herself from one man to the next. He couldn't forget she had offered to 'Netflix and chill' with Luke.

It didn't matter what had happened between them last night. Latifah didn't care about him. She didn't care about anyone.

He stormed out, returning to their table. Then he called Luke and told him to head back to Nigeria. There was no need for him to follow them because the journey was coming to an end. The BIS team would be Kojo's backup from here on.

Razi and Latifah returned to the restaurant.

Kojo stood, still unable to look at Latifah. He left her to eat and went outside.

Razi came up beside him as he strode to the car. "Take it easy on her."

He seemed to have picked up on Kojo's lousy mood, which annoyed Kojo more and confirmed there must be something between Razi and Latifah.

"Take it easy? She kidnapped Princess Isha. Have you forgotten?" Kojo rounded on his brother.

"Look, I know how it seems. But things aren't always so clear-cut or black and white."

"Things are very black and white from where I'm standing. She's a criminal and should pay for her crimes."

"In which case, you probably want me arrested as well. I've done some things that can be considered against the law in the name of my country."

"No. You are a government agent working to keep your country safe."

"So, you're saying when the state sanctions a kidnapping, it's okay. But when an individual does it, regardless of intentions, they're criminal. You're an idealist. I'm a realist. *Ti frè*, you need to climb off your high horse once in a while and see what the rest of us see."

Kojo's mouth dropped open. He didn't know what to say to his brother because the words hit hard. His life had always been so simple, so clear-cut. Now he was swimming in muddied waters, seemingly unable to make the right choices. Wanting a woman he shouldn't.

Raz sighed. "I'll see you around, *frè*. The BIS agents will shadow you until you reach your destination. Let me know if you need anything else."

"Okay." Kojo nodded.

Razi embraced him, took another look at him, and walked away.

Kojo let out a heavy breath, exhaustion weighing him down. Was he unrealistic by expecting people to adhere to specific moral codes?

He glanced up and saw Latifah exiting the restaurant. Pressing the hob, he unlocked and climbed into the car.

She climbed into the vehicle, settling in the front passenger seat. The confined space of the car made her scent fill his lungs. He itched to reach across and stroke her skin.

Then the image of her and his brother in the corridor replayed. His hands clenched around the steering wheel. He wouldn't be able to rest until he clarified the situation between her and his brother.

Of course, she tried to play her stupid games by not giving a direct answer. Unfortunately, the chip of ice in his veins just brought out his ruthless side. He threatened to throw her to the Bagumian authorities.

It was then he realised that his brother was correct.

Life wasn't always so black and white. He'd crossed the line with Latifah and was willing to travel it again.

Hence the reason he was in this hotel room, determined to satisfy his craving for her. He crossed the distance between them and loomed over her,

She tilted her head back and eyed him with a wary expression. He'd seen the confused look on her face last night as well when he'd bound her to the chair.

He took a deep breath, inhaling her scent of musk and sex.

"Still surprised, huh?" he tipped his lips up at a corner in a smirk.

"You got it," she commented, searching his face as if trying to read him.

He cocked his head. "There's only so much you can push a person before he snaps."

The late evening sun filtered through the edges of the partially drawn curtains. He hadn't turned on the lights.

Dark lashes feathered her cheeks as she closed her eyes. Her hair formed a halo around her face. Kojo would never describe her as angelic. Yet, in the dim light, she appeared demure, almost docile.

The look was deceptive. He knew differently. She was dangerous.

Still, he wanted more of her. Their passionate sexual session against the wall had only been to take the edge off his craving.

His desire for her was not diminished, and he was a long way from feeling satisfied.

Her head was tilted back, her sensuous neck exposed. One of the most erotic things he'd ever seen.

He accepted the invitation, lowered his body beside her, wrapped his hand around her throat. He didn't squeeze, just let the heaviness of his palm rest there.

Breath hitching, her lashes fluttered open, her pupils dilated, and a whimper spilled from her lips.

The sound went straight to his dick, turning it rock hard in seconds, making it chaff against his boxers.

"*Modi*, I could get addicted to the sounds you make when I touch you." He stood, tugging her up in the process.

Her throat rippled beneath his palm as she stared at him with the most fascinating brown eyes he'd ever seen.

Just staring into them made him want to lose inhibitions, lose himself in them.

The way her brows furrowed and she focused on him showed she was curious. Was she trying to figure him out? No doubt she was surprised the man right here seemed different from the one at the Lagos hotel the first day they'd met.

But he was intent on showing this side of himself. She should know that choosing to be non-provocative didn't make him a foot mat.

He stood there, waiting for her to say something, to tell him she didn't want to continue. She said nothing as if she'd accepted this part of him. As if she didn't know what to do with him when he was in control.

He glided his hand to the back of her neck, dipped his head and brushed his mouth to her. He kept his knee bent because her boots were didn't raise her to his level.

She stayed frozen, not responding.

He kept the kiss gentle, brushing from end to end, flicking his tongue against the seam of her mouth.

With a sigh of pleasure, she opened her mouth. A smile played on his lips, but he didn't indulge. Instead, he focused on tasting her, learning her flavour. There was a hint of salt and spice and something uniquely Latifah.

She was a robust meal all by herself. Nothing would ever taste like her.

Fingers reaching up to grip the front of his shirt, she sagged against him.

He reached down and cupped the luscious soft bum through the fabric of the skirt. She might have a slim waist, but her Africanity was evident in the bountiful breasts and ass.

Touching her ass triggered something wild inside him, and he wanted to see all of her.

He leaned back, breaking the kiss as he reached for the zip of her blouse and tugged it down. She raised her arms, allowing him to pull the top off and discard it to the floor.

Her eyes were dark amber with arousal and her lips swollen. Her breasts in black lace rose and fell with rapid breaths, the nipples poking through the flimsy material. Her skin was a tawny shade that he wanted to lick.

She reached back and unhooked the bra, letting the straps fall off her shoulders. She flung it away, leaving her top half exposed to his view.

From what he could see so far, she was beautiful. His heart galloped in his chest, and he didn't think he could keep still. But he let her carry on.

"Like what you see?" Her voice was sultry, the French accent more pronounced now. She tugged the side zip of the skirt and pushed it down, removing the panties in the process. She sat on the edge of the bed and unzipped the black knee-length boots. Putting them aside, she stood.

"You are perfection." He got the complete view of her. She was exactly what he needed right now.

Yet, he noticed some marks under her ribs. Gut tightening, he stepped around her, checking her back. The scarring continued. His stomach congealed.

He had sports injuries and healing marks on this body. Rugby was a physical sport. Wounds were part of it.

Yet, these were not recreational scars. Neither were they surgical.

Someone had hurt her. More than someone. Probably as a result of her risky job. He understood the danger. But guarding the princess was a walk-in-the-park compared to working as a covert agent. And since she was a freelancer, she probably didn't always have backup readily available to get her out of trouble.

His heart twisted, and his chest constricted.

He touched the circular mark on her back which looked like a healed bullet hole.

Her breath hitched, and he lowered to his knee and pressed his lips on it, tracing the edges of the welt reverently. He wanted to remove every pain associated with the wounds. Ached to claim them and own them. Just as he yearned to claim her and keep her.

Her breath hitched again, and she swivelled, bending to kiss him. It wasn't as gentle as the previous kiss. Instead, it was rough and demanding, as if she wanted him to forget about the wounds.

But he liked her response. Wanted her to show her emotions. To give them all to him.

He didn't want her hiding anything from him anymore.

He grabbed her hips. Lifting her off the floor.

She squealed as she wrapped her legs around his waist.

He lowered her onto the bed and covered her body with his, deepening the kiss. Taking a break to catch his breath, he slid his mouth along her jaw and neck. Cupping a breast with his palm, he sucked the tight bud into his mouth and lashed it with his tongue, taking long pulls.

Latifah gasped, clutching his head, holding it tight, digging her nails into his scalp,

He growled low in his throat, making her shudder from the vibrations. He bit into the nipple, and she cried out, her body arching into him.

He raised his head, soothing the sting and indentations with his tongue before turning his attention to the other breast and repeating the actions.

Her whimpers and body movements caused his heart to thump against his ribs.

He leaned back, standing to take his clothes off. Eyes locked on hers, he undid his shirt buttons, shrugged it off his shoulders and focused on his trousers. The buckle and zip were already undone. He tugged the waistband and shoved everything down, including his boxers, toeing his shoes too and stepping aside.

Then he turned his attention to her nakedness, drinking in her perfect body, scars and all, her flat belly, and the bare, slick pussy with trimmed bush. Her clit peeked through her labia, the flesh engorged, begging for his caress.

He covered Latifah with his body, tasting her mouth. She raised her head and met him halfway, opening for him and moaning when his hand returned to her breast.

He tilted his head, deepening the kiss, their bodies sliding and pushing against each other as lust rode his veins. Her moans were music to his ears. The way she kissed him was that of a lover, not just two people fucking.

If he didn't know better...

He pushed the thought aside. This wasn't the time for analysis. For the first time in days, he wouldn't think about why they'd met.

He focused on the ache in his dick, the need of his body. Stroked his palm down her belly and cupped her pussy. Parting the labia, he caressed her clit, and she arched into his touch, moaning into his mouth.

He caressed and cajoled, pinching and prodding until her body trembled and she cried out in pleasure. He bent down, dug into his discarded trousers, and pulled out a condom.

Latifah took it from him and tore the foil wrap before sliding the latex down his length, their gazes on each other, his breath locked tight.

The way she looked at him took his breath away. Her expression is soft. It's not just lust. There's something else. Something more profound. Something he couldn't explain.

It was as if she saw him. Really saw him.

His stomach flipped. She was his undoing.

He knelt between her leg, shoving them apart, baring everything, her dripping wet pussy and her puckered hole. His mouth watered, and he wanted a taste.

He slid his finger along her slit and then dip it inside as he lowered his mouth onto her clit.

Latifah moaned, canting her hip, sucking his finger deep into her warm wet core.

He pumped the finger, sliding another in, her juices coating them while rolling his tongue around her sensitive bundle of nerves. Then he withdrew the fingers, gliding wetness down to her puckered hole while pushing his thumb into her slit.

He circled the black hole at first, then slid the finger into the first knuckle. She didn't push him away. Instead, her body writhed, and her moans increased. He sucked hard on her clit, and orgasm flushed through her.

He didn't let her land, returning to his knees, gripping her hips, and slamming his dick inside her.

Another orgasm ripped out of her, rippling around his cock. He pulled out and slid in, her body rocking with his movements. She met him with every steady pumping motion, raising her legs to go deeper.

Soon sounds of flesh slapping flesh and moans and groans filled the air.

His breathing got heavier, and he knew he wasn't far off. So, he reached between them, fingering her clit. She came up, pulling his shoulders down and sealed their lips as another orgasm rolled through her.

Tension built inside him, and he drove his dick into her pussy several times before his release exploded through him with a low growl. He collapsed, head resting her shoulder as he drew in several deep breaths.

She didn't complain about his weight on her. Instead, wrapping her arms around him.

Satisfaction rolled through him, and he raised his head, giving her a brief kiss.

"I have to get rid of the condom," he said when he found his voice.

"Okay," she whispered, releasing him.

He pulled out and went to the bathroom. He discarded the condom and cleaned his dick before wetting a small towel. He returned to the bedroom and cleaned her. Then he ditched the towel in the bathroom.

When he came back into the room, she was under the sheets. He joined her.

She lay on her side facing him.

He stroked his palm down her arm. "How do you feel?"

"Good. Very good." She smiled, and it warmed his chest.

"Wonderful." He grinned. But his gaze fell on the scar under her breast. "How did you get this?"

He traced it with his fingertip. Wanting to know everything about her, he couldn't help the question.

She stayed silent for seconds that ticked into minutes, eyes closed. He didn't know if she would answer.

"That was a few years ago," she said finally. "I infiltrated a people-smuggling ring, and we rescued many young people. Some of the gang members were sent to jail. But they put a contract on my head. A hitman shot me and left me for dead. His mistake, though. Half-conscious, I managed to crawl to a street where someone found me and took me to the hospital. Twelve hours of surgery and four months of recovery. Another six months of laying low and plotting my revenge."

He gasped.

"And before you say it. Yes, it was revenge. I found the hitman. He had a penchant for picking up underage girls. I set a trap. He took the bait but got me instead. I slit his throat. It was good riddance to a paedophile."

He shifted, tugged her closer until her head rested on his chest. There was no way he would judge her for trying to stay alive.

She had put her life on the line to save others. She was a hero in his book regardless of what she'd done since.

This changed everything, though, because she was now on the wanted list.

"You know the BIS agents are here to arrest you," he said in a low voice. He had to do something to protect her.

"I know," She replied quietly.

"You'll go to jail, perhaps life imprisonment," he emphasised.

She puffed out a long breath. "I know."

He raised his head to stare at her face. "Are you not afraid?"

"I did what I did. Fear is not going to save me." She sounded resigned to her fate.

He gripped her face as his throat constricted.

"I'm afraid for you," he said in a hoarse voice. "I can't let you go to jail."

"Don't worry about me." She cupped his chin. "You're the one in trouble here. You lost the princess. You could be charged with treason. I'm trying to save you. Remember?"

"Hmmm." He lay down, caressing the soft skin of her back, her head back on his chest.

Yes, he was in trouble. But he would redeem himself by taking Princess Isha back home safely when he found her. However, Latifah was in a bigger mess. She would be arrested for kidnapping, taken to Bagumi, and tried in court. The result would be a lengthy prison term.

Perhaps, there was a way to save her. The Bagumian prosecutors would depend on Kojo's testimony to convict Latifah. They might also need Princess Isha's testimony. But if she is unharmed as Latifah promised, perhaps Kojo could intercede on

Latifah's behalf. The courts wouldn't compel him to testify against Latifah if she was his wife.

His muscles tensed, his pulse racing.

"What is it?" Latifah asked. She must have detected the change in him.

"I know a way to save you. A way for us to save ourselves." He scrubbed a hand over his head, trying to quell his agitation. This was crazy the more he thought about it. What other choice was there?

"You do? Tell me." She placed her hands on his chest and leaned her chin on them, staring up at him.

His thumping heart nearly punched a hole through his chest. "Marry me."

"What did you say?" She jerked upright, leaning on an elbow.

"I asked you to marry me." Her bewildered expression didn't fill him with confidence. Anxiety made his stomach roll. He'd never proposed to anyone. Hadn't thought doing it would be so nerve-racking. He swallowed and continued when she said nothing. "As your husband, I can't incriminate you. I can't be forced to testify against you."

"Are you out of your mind? They could accuse you of being an accomplice if we get married." She really didn't look pleased with his suggestion.

His heart fell. Was marrying him really such a terrible idea? They'd known each other for a short while. Still, somehow, he would like to take this thing between them beyond just sex.

He imagined waiting for her to return from one of her missions. Pictured having her in bed with him and waking with her every morning while she was home.

Of course, if Princess Isha married Kweku, Kojo would move to Wanai with her. If he still had a job. Then Latifah wouldn't have to relocate to Bagumi.

Nevertheless, if they maintain the status quo, he would only see Latifah during prison visits.

His chest constricted. He couldn't let it happen. "Marrying me will give you immunity, and the authorities might be more lenient."

She rolled off the bed and snatched her clothes from the floor. "No. I got you into this mess in the first place. I'm not going to drag you deeper into it."

He sat up, putting his feet on the carpet. "If you won't marry me to save yourself, then marry me because I care about you and want to commit my future to you. Marry me because I want to love you, cherie."

Sure, his life was boring compared to her exciting adventures. And he wasn't the most eligible bachelor around. Still, he had things going for him. He was healthy, had a good job and had great investments. He knew how to commit himself fully to the care of the lady in his life. Moreover, being a royal guard gave him privileges that would extend to her.

"You want to love me? Now I know you're crazy." She froze, clutching the clothes to her chest. "Have you not seen the impact of my lifestyle. Seen the scars on my body. And for your information, I've been married before. He didn't want me when he found out that I wouldn't come home every night. I'm not going to give up what I do."

He stood and walked towards her, sensing an opportunity. "I don't care if you've been married before as long as you're free to marry me now. Your ex didn't appreciate you. That's my gain. Maybe it takes a crazy person to truly appreciate you. I'm that person. I'm not asking you for much. Just let me be yours. Let me protect you the way I can."

"Damn. You really mean it." Her eyes shimmered with unshed tears.

"I do," he said solemnly, straining not to touch her.

"Okay. On one condition. It has to stay secret until the situation with the princess is resolved."

"Deal."

"Great. I know an imam who will marry us at short notice."

He swooped her up and sealed it with a kiss.

Chapter 12

Two days later, Latifah and Kojo were back in the car and had just crossed the fourth border in as many days. Travelling into Wanai proved the most difficult of the countries they'd been in recently.

The Wanaian government scrutinised travellers thoroughly, only allowing Wanai citizens to return to the country due to the ongoing unrest in the Ganuri region. Those going beyond Wanaian borders were redirected through neighbouring nations like Burkina Faso

Kojo was cleared for entry when he showed the newly minted marriage certificate proving he married a Wanaian citizen.

Latifah still couldn't believe that she was married to him. Talk about a whirlwind romance. A few days ago, it had seemed like he hated her. They had been adversaries. Now they were spouses.

She still didn't think it was a good idea, considering the trouble he could get into because of her. But she hadn't been able to reject his beautiful heartfelt proposal.

He was a decent, compassionate, loving human being, and she didn't know how she could have gotten so lucky.

After her first marriage ended, she'd resorted to brief affairs. None of the men had wanted anything permanent with her, which had suited her. None of them really understood the secrecy involved in her life, and she never told them what she did for a living.

Kojo had looked inside her, seen all her flaws, all her baggage and still wanted her.

She only hoped she could live up to his expectations, and his feelings would remain the same when the harsh realities of their lives kicked in.

On her part, she cared about him. It was the reason she wanted to save him from trouble and distress by taking him to see the princess in Wanai.

But love? She'd only known him for less than a week.

How long did it take for people to fall in love?

She'd never given her heart to anyone since her husband. She didn't even remember what romantic love felt like.

Now each time she glanced at Kojo as he drove, butterflies fluttered in her belly. Warmth bloomed across her chest.

He'd surprised her yesterday at the wedding by arranging for Razi and Luke to be witnesses. He'd made the necessary arrangements, and they'd celebrated afterwards before Razi had to catch a return flight to Bagumi. Luke had driven back to Lagos this morning.

Kojo looked at her, a grin on his face. "Why are you smiling?"

"You're smiling too." She giggled, sounding like a teen. It was crazy how light and floaty she was around him. He made her feel young and carefree.

"I'm grinning because you're my wife." He reached out and held her hand.

She lifted their joined hands to her lips and kissed his knuckles. "I'm excited about what the future holds for us."

"So am I." He tugged her hand and reciprocated the kiss, brushing his lips on the back of her hand.

"Think about all the adventures we'll have together."

"Adventures, yes. But I would be just happy to have you home and in my bed."

"Where would home be? Bagumi or Wanai?" They hadn't even thought about those details. At the moment, she lived in Wanai and him in Bagumi. She didn't mind setting up a home in his country. But her current work was in Wanai. Her cousin needed her to finish what they'd started.

"Home is wherever you are," he said, glancing at her

"Oh. You are sweet." She reached across and squeezed his arm. "But that doesn't help with the practicalities. You work in Bagumi."

He grimaced. "That's if I still have a job after all of this."

She kissed his hand again to reassure him. "You can come and work in Wanai for me. Ever saw the new movie 'The Hitman's Bodyguard'? You could become the spy's bodyguard."

He chuckled, the sound rich and warm. "That sounds like fun. Do I get six weeks paid holiday and a wardrobe allowance?"

Her lips widened. "Well, you get to fuck your principal whenever you wish."

"Deal." He winked at her.

And it was her turn to giggle. It looked like they were going to get on brilliantly. They could really be the perfect fit and not just for sex.

She noticed the sign for another service stop. "Can you stop? I need to use the ladies."

"Okay. I'll get some fuel while you're in there." He slowed and pulled into the petrol station before stopping.

Latifah noticed another car pull up at a stall a few meters in front of them. Her spine prickled. She'd seen the car following them. But it wasn't the BIS agents. Kojo had dismissed the agents yesterday before the wedding. So they had left.

These ones were different. Perhaps the same ones that had followed them from Lagos, and she'd lost track of them in Cotonou.

She would find a way to evade them when they got back on the road. She walked the restaurant and straight to the back where they had the toilets. Her neck prickled with the sensation of being watched. She entered the ladies, used a cubicle. When she came out, someone shoved a hand over her mouth.

"Don't move," the male voice said.

To hell with that. She wasn't letting any person manhandle her. The only one who'd earned the privilege was Kojo.

She swung her elbow, catching him in the ribs, sending him crashing against a cubicle door. He didn't let go, though, grabbing her around the waist.

A woman opened the door, saw them, and ran out in fear.

Latifah lifted her legs, using him as an anchor to brace against the wall and shove back. He hit his head against the door frame, grunted and loosened his grip. She took advantage, stomping her boot into his knee. He groaned and crumpled.

The door swung open, and another man entered. He seemed shocked to find his friend on the floor. Before he could react, she took a running jump and landed a kick in his groin, sending him into a groaning ball on the floor.

"What the hell." Kojo stepped in as the man next to him tried to stand. He seemed to read the situation, punched the man in the gut, and he collapsed again.

Kojo walked over and wrapped his arms around her. His cocoon was comforting. "Are you hurt?"

He leaned back, searching for injuries.

"No. I'm fine." She went to the sink and ran the tap quickly, cleaning her hands. He grabbed some paper towels for her, and she dabbed her face. "We need to leave."

"Sure." He took her hand and opened the door.

A man in the restaurant uniform approached. "What's going on here?"

"There are men in your restaurant harassing women in the ladies' bathroom. They are in there,"

Kojo said, but he didn't stop moving until they were outside the restaurant.

When they go to the car park, Latifah spoke, "That's their car, the grey SUV. We can't have them following us to the destination."

"What do you want to do?" Kojo frowned, his body going into alert mode.

"Keep a lookout while I can slash their tyres, so they don't follow."

"Okay. You ready?"

"Yeah." She kissed him quickly.

Kojo watched the restaurant while Latifah kept low and crept to the car. She bent like she was picking something from the ground, pulled out the knife tucked into her boot and jammed it into the rear wheel, making sure to cut through the tube so it would be unrepairable.

Then she hurried back and got into their car.

Kojo glanced around and followed her back to the car. He climbed in and started the engine, and pulled away, driving fast in a screech of wheels. "Are you okay?"

"Yes." She glanced back, checking to see if the men who'd attacked her were following. It seemed they were not out of the restaurant yet. When they did, it would take them a while to change the deflated tyre.

She grinned and turned back with relief. "So, how did you know to come check for me?"

"You took too long. I think you're right. You need someone watching over you."

Warmth bloomed across her chest. When he talked like that, it was easy to fall in love with him.

She laughed. "Exactly. I need a personal bodyguard."

"Hang on, though. If those men followed us from Nigeria, they have to be Kweku's minions."

"Yep. And it wasn't good news for them to follow us. Unfortunately, Wanai is Kweku's territory. We must get off this highway soon to avoid getting caught at checkpoints."

"Okay. Let me know where to go."

"At the next junction, follow the left exit," she said, rubbing a hand over her face. "I must remember to get some unripe plantain for my aunt before we get there. She loves them. By the way, remember how I once told you that it was exciting to get blown while you're driving. Want to try it."

He glanced at her, eyes smouldering. "Cherie, you should know I'm not *that* adventurous. I'll wait until I don't risk killing you before you can blow me."

"That's a deal, big guy. I'm going to hold you to it."

***

Two hours later, Latifah directed Kojo as he drove up the slope leading to the Bassong residence in Boma. He beeped the horn as they pulled up outside the wrought-iron gates.

One of the security guards carrying a weapon came out of the side entrance.

Latifah leaned out of the window and ordered. "Open the gates."

"Yes, madam," he replied and rushed inside.

A few seconds later, metals grated as the locks were disengaged and the barrier pulled aside.

"Just find a spot under the carport," she said as Kojo drove onto the stone-paved driveway. He pulled to a stop beside her aunt's old Mercedes. The SUVs her cousin and his team used were not in their usual spots. Confirmation that he'd left for his trip with the princess and hadn't returned.

Her conscience prickled because she hadn't told Kojo about Princess Isha going on a trip with Professor Bassong. He would think that she had been trying to deceive him when she'd merely forgotten because of everything that had happened while they'd been in Accra.

Shit.

No other choice. She had to tell him now before he went into the house, thinking he would see the princess today.

"Big guy." She unclipped her seatbelt and twisted in the seat. "Don't get mad, okay. I'm not trying to trick you. But Princess Isha is not here."

He narrowed his eyes and glanced around. "What do you mean she's not here? Isn't this the location she was taken?"

"Yes, it is. This is my cousin's house, and she was brought here. But she went on a trip with my cousin. He—"

"On a trip? You kidnap her, and now she's on a trip? To think I believed you. Fooled twice. How foolish can I get?" He shoved the door and stepped out only to be confronted with Solomon, pointing a gun at his face.

"Raise your hands!" Her adopted cousin shouted.

"What the hell." Latifah jumped out of the car, ran to the other side, and stepped in front of Kojo, shielding him with her body. "Sol, what the fuck are you doing?"

Solomon still had the gun levelled at Kojo's head. He was taller than her and was a crack shot. She had no doubt he would put a bullet in Kojo if he wanted. "I should ask you the same. We're in the middle of a bloody war, and you brought him here?"

"I'm here for the princess," Kojo bit out.

Latifah glanced at him and swallowed. She stepped backwards, trying to shuffle him away from the potential bullet. But the stubborn man didn't budge. "He's my guest."

Solomon's gaze bounced between Kojo and her and returned to her husband. "Your guest. Are you out of your mind? He could be a Doona spy."

"He's not. You have to take my word for it if it still means anything around here," she snapped. It was on the tip of her tongue to reveal their married status. But she'd promised to keep it a secret. So, she swallowed again.

Solomon huffed out a breath. He still didn't look convinced but lowered his weapon.

"Where is the princess?" Kojo bit out, stepping around Latifah.

Solomon just turned and walked towards the front door of the house, ignoring him.

"If any of you have hurt her—"

Latifah swivelled and shoved Kojo against the car, cutting off his rant. She pressed against him, rising on her toes, so her mouth was inches from his.

"Just stop," she said against his lips. "I swore to you that nothing bad happened to the princess. I married you. I just fucking stood up to my cousin for you. And still, you will not trust me. You leave me no other choice—"

He cupped her face, lowered his head, and kissed her, cutting her off. Right under the carport outside her aunt's house, with the security personnel watching. This was the most un-Kojo thing to do. Public displays were not his thing. Yet here he was doing it.

And there could only be one reason. He cared about her, and he wanted to stay married.

Her heart melted. She'd never thought she was the marrying kind. Yet, she knew she would not give up this man. Not for the moon or the stars. Not for anyone.

He raised his head and whispered against her lips. "I trust you. I'm never letting you go, cherie."

"Neither am I, big guy. You've got me for life."

"Good. Now, are you going to introduce me to your aunt?"

"Of course. This way." She led him towards the front entrance and into the house to begin yet another adventure.

Author's Note

Thank you for reading Saving Her Guard. If you enjoyed this story please leave a review on the site of purchase.

Saving Her Guard was always meant to fill the gap and answer the question of what happened between Kojo and Latifah after Princess Isha was abducted and before they arrived in Wanai. It is a steamy, romantic, road trip story.

To find out what happens after they get to Wanai, read His Captive Princess (Royal House of Saene, book 3).

To find out what happens to Kweku Doona, read His Captive Princess and The Tainted Prince (Royal House of Saene, book 6)

Also, Razi Hamadou (Kojo's brother) shows up in The Tainted Prince.

His Captive Princess is out now.

The Tainted Prince is out 30th September 2021

To find out about my upcoming book releases and giveaways, sign up for my newsletter.

I would also love to connect with you on social media. You can find me on Facebook, Twitter and Instagram.

www.kirutaye.com

Continue reading for the prologue from The Tainted Prince by Kiru Taye.

Prologue — The Tainted Prince

CROWN PRINCE Zawadi Saene's life seemed to be ruled by meetings.

Since his father, King Ibrahim Aziz Saene, ruler of the Bagumi Kingdom, had a coronary seizure a year ago, Zawadi as first-in-line to the throne had taken on more responsibilities.

And it seemed more responsibilities equated with more meetings. Meetings with national ministers. Meetings with foreign dignitaries and diplomats. Meetings with lawmakers. Meetings with family. And on and on it went.

Like the family conference he'd been invited to attend this afternoon*n in his father's private reception room.

The active senior members of the Royal House of Saene met every quarter to discuss policy and governance issues concerning the kingdom.

Private family get-togethers were infrequent and seemed to be limited to special occasions, these days. His siblings were all adults, living their lives even while committed to duties as serving members of the Royal House.

Zawadi saw his father weekly for briefings. Although the king was semi-retired, he liked to stay up to date on matters of state. That had been one of the caveats to his semi-retirement.

This wasn't one of those meetings he shared with his father on a Friday morning before their trip to the mosque located in the expansive palace grounds. His assistant had informed him of the impromptu insertion into his schedule earlier.

He walked along the endless vaulted corridors of Darusa Palace lit by sunlight through French windows or domed multihued skylights, past stationary uniformed guards and scampering liveried servants. DP as they fondly referred to the king's formal residence was made up of sprawling building connected by corridors and hidden passages.

He took a shortcut through a sun-drenched interior courtyard, a warm breeze flicking his jacket lapel. Pink bougainvillea covered a wall, the air scented by roses bushes. That was another noteworthy feature—the magnificent gardens surrounding the buildings.

As he walked through another set of double doors, he spotted his immediate younger brother, Prince Azikiwe, otherwise known as Zik to his siblings, in the corridor heading towards their father's private quarters.

"What's going on?" Zawadi asked as he levelled up with Zik.

Zik grimaced. "Something came up and I called an emergency meeting."

So, his brother was the reason for the conference.

"Are Zareb and Zediah joining us?" he asked, stopping briefly outside the doors to the king's private reception room.

"No. This is a sensitive diplomatic issue," Zik replied.

Well, that ruled out the twins, who would rather gouge their eyes out than discuss diplomacy, for different reasons. Zareb was on the 'bludgeon them into submission' end of the spectrum while Zediah would rather sit and drink tea with the opponents. As if drinking tea solved the world's problems. Then again, neither was 'hitting the enemy where it hurts' always a viable solution.

Zawadi shook his head in amusement at the thought as the guard announced him and his brother.

He stepped into the large reception room first, followed by Zik.

Antique paintings, metal and wooden sculptures documenting the history of Bagumi lined the white walls. A large hand-woven rug covered the aisle from the door to the platform with three hand-carved heavy wooden chairs. The one in the middle was embedded with gemstones it to signify the status of the grey-haired man who sat in its regal glory.

His flowing robe had colourful patterns representing the colours of the gems extracted from the Bagumian mines.

The consorts sat on either of him—to the right Queen Zulekha, the first wife, and Zawadi's mother. On the left Queen Sapphire, Zik's mother. They spoke in low voices.

Zawadi and Zik approached the dais and prostrated, a show of submission to their parents.

King Ibrahim might be their father but he was also *the king*.

"Long live King Ibrahim and The Royal House of Saene," they said together.

"Rise, my sons," his father's voice boomed. He leaned forward and pulled Zawadi into a hug first, then Zik.

Zawadi would admit he was not a huge hugger, but these tactile moments with his parents were priceless. He did the rounds, hugging the two queens as well.

"Mama, is that a new dress?" Zik said. "The fabric is gorgeous."

Zawadi glanced over at his brother who was brushing the arm of Queen Zulekha's blue gown.

The senior consort's eyes sparkled as she beamed a smile at his sibling. "Yes, it is. The tailor delivered it yesterday and I'm wearing it for the first time. Thank you."

His brother kissed the queen on the cheek.

"You're welcome, Mama." Zik pulled up a chair beside Queen Sapphire. He met Zawadi's gaze and winked.

Zawadi shook his head as he lowered his body into an armchair, hiding his smile.

He would admit Zik had this charming personality locked down. Zawadi hadn't met any person whom Zik couldn't charm. Especially women. He regularly had the queens eating out of his palm, even the usually shrewd Queen Zulekha seemed to turn into a blushing lady when he turned his attention to her.

That was one thing he would give his brother. Zik paid attention to things Zawadi would consider trivial. Like noticing the queen's new outfit.

While the dress was lovely, Zawadi hadn't known it was new. It wasn't the kind of detail he would care to note, except when someone else pointed it out.

Anyway, if his brother was trying to keep Queen Zulekha sweet, then there must be something grave he wanted to discuss. Which brought them to why they were here.

A servant approached the other side of the bank of chairs and bent to whisper in Zik's ear.

Zik nodded and the man stepped back towards the side where a projector had been set up.

"Something was brought to my attention that I think you should all see," Zik said. "I won't say anymore until you have watched the video. May I play it?"

"Sure. Go ahead," the king confirmed.

Zik turned the servant and nodded.

The lights dimmed, the place lit only by the light from the projector which turned the far wall into a giant screen.. As this was an internal chamber, there were no exterior windows.

Silence descended into the room as the images rolled across the screen that Zawadi could only describe as human devastation—demolished buildings, piles of dead bodies, mass graves, refugee camps.

Zawadi's mind went to all the current locations of conflict in the continent.

Was that Darfur, South Sudan? Or the Central African Republic? Perhaps DRC or Angola?

Whatever the location, his stomach hardened and his chest tightened painfully.

These were Africans. Fellow Africans.

His grief was also tainted by anger. Anger because those in charge of the location obviously did not understand the responsibility of power. True leadership was about the greater good and should never be about personal gain. It wasn't about egos.

Yet many who wielded power didn't seem to understand or simply didn't care.

From when he'd been a boy he'd been taught about power and prepared for leadership. Prepared to rule the Kingdom of Bagumi. That was his duty. He would not fail.

He would be damned if he would fail the citizens of this country, by giving into personal whims or something unnecessary.

He accepted that Bagumi and the welfare of its citizens came first about everything else.

But who was going to fight for the aggrieved citizens of the country being shown on screen? The Royal House of Saene had always intervened where possible during conflicts especially in West Africa. In the past, they'd sent diplomats, brokered peace deals, and had brought warring factions to the table.

But this didn't exactly look like war.

At least there was no mention of war in the commentary.

They talked about random attacks against unarmed civilians.

Hang on. A name on the commentary caught his attention. And another one.

And he knew something was wrong.

Zawadi tilted his head and squinted under the flashing light to glare at his brother sitting across the aisle.

As if he was expecting Zawadi's reaction, Zik stared at him boldly.

What was his brother playing at? Was he trying to ambush Zawadi? For what purpose?

The lights came on as silence descended when the projection stopped.

Zawadi didn't wait. He couldn't wait.

"Azikiwe, what game are you playing?" Zawadi asked, keeping a tight hold on the anger bubbling inside.

"This is no game, brother," his sibling replied.

"Then that footage must have been doctored ... Fake news."

"I'm afraid not. That is as real as they come. I got it from a reliable source."

Zawadi shook his head. "No. Somebody is trying to stir trouble. You can't trust everything you see. They have video altering software that distort the truth."

"If we can't trust the video it means we can't trust the Bagumi Intelligence Service."

"What?" asked Zawadi in shock,

The queens gasped.

"Azikiwe, explain yourself," the king ordered.

"Your majesty," Zik started. "About a month ago, I received credible information about the systematic violation of human rights of the people of the Ganuri region of the Wanai Republic. Wanting to verify things before I could present the information to you, I commissioned the Bagumi Intelligence Service to investigate to verify the validity of the allegations."

"On whose authority?" the king asked the question at the top of Zawadi's lips.

His brother could have triggered an international crisis with their neighbour by sending spies into Wanai. There could still be repercussions from that video alone.

"Mine, Your Majesty. I thought it was best to keep you and Zawadi out of the loop in case something went wrong. That way you would have plausible deniability and your integrity would not be compromised. And I would take the blame alone."

Okay. Zik had thought it through and had been willing to bear the consequences.

Still.

"And when did you get the video?"

"The intelligence officers returned last week and I had a meeting with them where I watched the footage."

"Hang on. You've been sitting on this information for a week?" This was getting worse.

What excuse would his brother come up with this time?

"I had to travel to Wanai the day after I watched the video. As you were aware, our sister Isha was visiting Kweku, her fiancé at the time. Her immediate safety was important at the time and I had to extract her securely. Once we returned other matters grabbed by attention. This was the earliest opportunity to discuss it with the rest of you."

What Zik had omitted was that Isha had been abducted by her ex-lover, her old university lecturer who was now a terrorist and had taken her to Wanai. Kweku had rescued her from the man and taken her to the presidential palace in Wanai where Zik had picked her and brought her home.

But they hadn't informed their father about the abduction. Zawadi would not mention it now. He didn't need to aggravate the old man or trigger another heart attack since Isha was now home and well.

A palace guard approached and spoke to Zik in a low voice.

"Excuse me for a moment," Zik said before following the man out of the door.

"Do you really think that footage is fake?" Queen Zulekha asked in a sober tone.

"I don't know," Zawadi replied. "Our intelligence service would not create fake videos. For what purpose?"

"No. Our intelligence service would not stoop to such levels. They know it would be easy to test the video for veracity. And the culprit would pay a heavy price."

"Which leaves a troubling reality," the king said. "Our allies have not been frank with us. According to that report, Kweku Doona is responsible for many of the atrocities."

"I am shocked, Your Majesty. And you will have to forgive me for not rushing to condemn him until I can double check the evidence."

He needed undeniable, irrefutable evidence before he could condemn a man he'd called his friend for over fifteen years.

He'd known Kweku Doona since they were at the military academy as teenagers. As both first sons of heads of states, they'd become fast friends and had been on adventures together.

In recent times, they'd assumed greater governance roles and more responsibility which meant they didn't see each other as often anymore. But they kept in touch by phone and other messaging services regularly.

About a year ago, Kweku and Isha got engaged.

Zawadi was looking forward to cementing his friendship with Kweku by becoming brothers in law.

Talk about the devil.

His sister, Isha walked into the reception room, hand in hand with a man whom Zawadi didn't recognise at first.

Zawadi's body tensed and he ground his teeth as recognition dawned.

Professor Bassong? How did that terrorist get into the palace? Where the hell was Zareb? Did he know about this?

As Isha greeted their parents, Mr Bassong who stood in the middle of the aisle.

Zawadi glared at the man, hands balled by his sides.

He wanted to smash the man's face in for what he did to Isha when she was a young student. Hell, he wanted to lock the man up and throw away the key.

Imagine a lecturer seducing his student. That's what the man had done to Isha. She hadn't even been out of her teen years when the two had met. Mr Bassong was ten years older, had been the lecturer in a position of power and he had abused that power by preying on Isha, seducing her, and then abandoning her.

Such immoral men shouldn't be allowed to walk around freely.

Now, here he was in the palace, apparently with Isha's consent. What did Isha see in such a man? Didn't she know that the man probably did the same things to other women?

Worse the man had become the leader of a terrorist organisation.

If Zawadi had been a betting man, he would gamble that all the atrocities they had just watched in that video was due to Mr Bassong and his militia, the MLG.

Isha turned to him, saying hello.

"I was not aware that you had a guest." Zawadi didn't hid his displeasure at seeing her former lecturer in their midst.

Isha seemed to take that as her cue to introduce the professor, who in turn prostrated before the king.

Zawadi jerked back in surprise. He hadn't been expecting that. Even Kweku had never fully prostrated, only choosing to bow before the king.

It seemed the man was here on a charm offensive. Hopefully, the king would see through the act.

But things went in a different direction and the king gave the man an audience, allowing him to state his case with Isha reminding everyone about the situation in Ganuri.

"Oh, yes," Queen Sapphire said. "Those were horrible scenes. Imagine all those women and children in those camps. We must do something about it."

"We are, Mum," Isha said. "We've submitted a case file to the International Criminal Courts who have started their investigations."

"Does Kweku know about this?" Zawadi asked, unable to contain the contempt from his siblings. They had bypassed him, bypassed protocol, and already filed a case with the ICC. Azikiwe and Isha had pulled some stunts in the past. But this was the worst. How dare they?

"Yes, he does. He and his father are the accused."

Zawadi flipped. He'd heard enough of the bullshit. "You can't be serious. The only person guilty of a crime is the terrorist you brought into this palace." He pointed at Zain. "Papa, that man is the lecturer Isha had an affair with when she was in London. He is also the leader of the separatist group fighting to split from Wanai."

"No, it's not true. He's not a terrorist." Isha stepped down to stand beside Zain.

Of course, his sister would deny it. Like she hadn't been shacked up with the man for the past month when she should have been preparing for her wedding to Kweku.

Mr Bassong took Isha's hand. Right there in front of everyone.

Zawadi loved his sister. But Almighty give him strength. Did she not have any shame? How could she have rekindled her doomed love affair with the man only weeks to her wedding.

There were certain behaviours not allowed in the presence of the king. No public displays. And holding hands with a man you were not engaged to was certainly one of them.

Why couldn't Isha obey simple rules?

Zawadi wanted to walk down the dais and separate the two. But the man was pleading for the king's forgiveness about his affair with Isha when she'd been a student and asking for their father's permission to marry her now.

What an effrontery. The man had *cajones* after what he'd done.

"That may be so, young man," the king said. "But no terrorist is going to marry my daughter."

Thank goodness their father wasn't easily swayed by talk.

"Your Majesty, I swear to you on my life that I have never committed any of the crimes that Doona accuses me of. Prince Azikiwe sent spies into Ganuri to document the events. If he found any evidence of members of my group persecuting the citizens, I'm sure he would have presented them to you today."

"That's true, Papa." Zik joined Isha and Mr Bassong on the aisle. "The intelligence officers that went into Ganuri found no evidence of crimes committed by the MLG. Instead, the group have provided safe zones and shelter for the people who have been attacked. There is genocide going on, and all fingers point to Doona, especially Kweku who has been arresting and torturing the people campaigning for independence."

The hits kept coming. Now, Zik was blaming Kweku for the atrocities? What was wrong with his siblings? Kweku was no angel but this was farfetched.

But thing flew away from him.

Before Zawadi knew what was going on their father was proclaiming that there would be a wedding between Isha and Mr Bassong and everyone stood to congratulate the new couple.

Zawadi stood still reeling from the shock when Zik came up to him and patted his shoulder. "Don't take this personal. You should know Isha well enough. When she wants something, she will move Heaven and Hell to make it happen."

"But how can you accept him so readily after what he did to her?" Zawadi tilted his head in Mr Bassong's direction.

Zik shrugged. "I accept him because I know how much Isha loves him."

"Even if he's not good enough for her?" Zawadi just couldn't get his head around such whimsiness.

"Grandma used to say that true love is unconditional. The heart yearns for whom it yearns." There was a forlorn expression in Zik's eyes that Zawadi had never seen before. Then the man shook his head, wiping the expression. "Maybe one day you'll understand the idiom."

Zawadi nearly laughed. He would never be so besotted that he would be able to tell right from wrong. He didn't have his head in the clouds.

There was already a woman in his life whom he cared for and loved. Soon they would be married and they would live happily ever after just like his parents.

Continue reading for chapter one from Scar's Redemption by Kiru Taye.

Chapter One - <u>Scar's Redemption</u>

Sweat rolled down Pacca Zhuri's skin. The wavy corrugated iron roof of the corn-coloured brick house was too far away to provide any shade, and the nearest tree was at the back of the building.

Ignoring the large droplets mixing with dust at her feet, she concentrated on laying out the coloured stones in the outlined mosaic pattern. Between school and other chores, it had taken weeks to reach this final phase. Still, she was determined to finish everything before her mother arrived home.

Mama was the most important person in her life and today was her birthday.

Pacca couldn't afford to take a bus to the nearest town so she could visit one of the brightly lit supermarkets to buy a present. Neither could she spend the little fund available at the local market.

Using ingenuity and her hands, she had crafted a gift instead.

Mama was house-proud. As a busy nurse and midwife who ran the local clinic, she rarely had time for herself—tending to residents and sometimes travelling to other places. With no losses recorded, she'd assisted in the safe deliveries of a generation of children in the small town and beyond, earning a reputation of having been blessed by the gods.

When not at work, Mama tended the garden. The land at the back of the house had been turned into a vegetable and herb farm.

However, Pacca had decided to convert the front lawn into a flowered patio.

"Are we going to eat flowers?" her mother had queried.

"No. But the garden will look pretty, maybe as pretty as you, Mama," she'd replied.

Mama's laughter echoed and filled Pacca with warmth and joy.

"You are such a sweet talker. In my next life, I will choose you as my daughter."

"And I will choose you as my mother."

She grinned and hugged her parent, who acted as both mother and father. She had no recollections of the man who sired her as he'd been a soldier killed in an ambush before she'd been born. Mama often said Pacca had her father's spirit, which would explain why she behaved like a boy sometimes.

To accomplish her goal for the front yard, Pacca had taken books about landscaping from the school library and had been able to make a rough sketch. Over the weeks, she'd made or borrowed items. Her friend, who worked as a part-time labourer, brought leftover paints sourced from different building sites. She even reclaimed wood from neighbours' old thrown-away furniture.

While her mother had seen the work in progress, she hadn't witnessed this final installation. Painting the individual stones and laying them out in the correct arrangement was the trickiest and most tasking aspect. But the multi-coloured mosaic added vibrancy and energy to the final display, and she couldn't wait to reveal it.

She lifted the corner of her yellow T-shirt and wiped the sweat on her eyebrows while stones prodded her bare knees. The knee-length baggy shorts helped her move freely while doing her chores.

However, when she cleaned up later, she would change into a white-with-blue-polka-dots sundress to please Mama.

Some people believed a girl shouldn't wear shorts or trousers.

The first time Pacca had picked a pair of shorts from the market stall, her mother hadn't refused. A few townsfolk made comments about the 'inappropriate' clothing, and Mama had laughed them off. No one had pushed the issue. Who would dare to piss off the one person they would call during a health emergency?

"How easily people forget their history?" Mama had said. "Our ancestors dressed differently from the way we dress today. Fashion is guaranteed to change."

Pacca laughed. "What do you know about fashion?"

Mama winked at her. "I was young once, you know. I wasn't always your Mama."

Pacca's lips widened with her smile at the memory.

A warm wind blew and fluttered the blades of the green grassland to her left.

Thunder rumbled in the distance.

Not rain. Not now.

She glanced up. The horizon stayed clear, with no visible clouds.

Returning her attention to the mosaic pattern, she lifted a stone. The ground beneath her knees quaked.

Sounds of thunder and yet no dark clouds or flashes of lightning? Now the earth seemed to tremble.

What was going on?

Her curious nature made her push off and stand. She walked down the widened track leading past other houses and headed toward the main tarred road, which ran through the middle of the town. Neighbours, old and young, meandered towards the mysterious loud noises.

In the distance, a dust storm darkened the atmosphere, swirling and churning. Visible heat waves rose from the tarmac. The trembling hardened and roared, like the wild creatures that stalked the forests. The curtain of dust parted, revealing massive mechanical objects trundling down the road.

"Pacca, run!"

She whipped around when someone shouted her name, only to be confronted by a vision of red as a man imploded and tumbled onto the earth.

Pacca froze, eyes bulging. She'd never seen anything like it before.

A scream bubbled in her throat but stayed trapped. It seemed her fifteen-year-old brain couldn't process the danger.

A loud explosion behind Pacca ripped an anguished cry from her mouth and triggered her feet into motion. She stumbled and abandoned her flip-flops.

Balls of flames fired from armoured tanks crashed into buildings, rending earth and plants, setting everything ablaze.

Neighbours and friends ran, cried, and fell.

Pacca stopped to help a woman with a baby only to scream when what looked like a gleaming metal ball ripped through mother and child.

Tears welled, blurring Pacca's vision as everything around her seemed to crumble and burn.

The noise from machine-gun fire and grenades mixed with the constant rumble of the monster trucks.

Pacca scrabbled along with one thought in mind. *Find Mama.*

She meandered behind the back of the single-level brick houses, hiding from the men carrying blood-soaked machetes. Rounding the corner, she halted in front of her home and glanced around to check for any intruders.

"Pacca!"

She swivelled at the sound of her name and saw Mama running from the opposite direction.

"Mama," she shouted and hurried towards her parent.

"I'm so glad you're okay." Her mother hugged her tight. "I had to come and find you as soon we cleared everyone out of the clinic. Come on. We need to hide in the bush."

They ran towards the back of the house.

Smoke filled the sky. Several shots rang out.

Mama's hand slipped, and she tumbled onto the ground.

Pacca's scream splintered the air, and her knees gave way. She tugged her mother, whose blue uniform became stained with a rapidly spreading patch of red, her unseeing eyes fixed upwards.

"No!" A boulder of pain sat in her chest, crushing it, and she struggled to breathe. This couldn't happen. Mama couldn't be dead. Today was her birthday. Pacca still hadn't shown her the gift she'd made. "Mama, get up. You'll love your present."

She cradled the body to her chest as tears streaked down her cheeks. Her body grew hot and cold.

"Get up," someone ordered.

Pacca looked up to find she was surrounded by two men in green camouflage uniforms.

The sight of the weapons across their shoulders triggered rage, not fear.

Pounding roared in her ears. Her vision clouded. Her palms clenched and unclenched.

These men had killed Mama. They'd ruined her special day.

Mama, who never hurt anyone.

Who would take care of pregnant women and babies now?

One of the militants leaned over her, hand extended, teeth bared. "I say, get up."

Pacca jerked out of his reach and braced herself. Propelled by anger, she drove her head into his groin, a trick she'd learnt after she realised how sensitive the area was for men.

The man groaned in agony and doubled over. His colleague back-handed Pacca and the metallic taste of blood filled her mouth.

Suddenly dark clouds appeared overhead, and the heavens opened, drenching everything.

The militants dragged her towards the house, probably seeking shelter from the downpour.

Unwilling to be a docile victim, she kicked and clawed, tearing flesh, which seemed to enrage them. She didn't care if they killed her, but she wouldn't beg.

One man tugged at her T-shirt while the other held her down. The wet fabric proved challenging to rip, and he pulled a dagger out.

Suddenly the man on top was yanked by a great force and flew across the garden onto a broken fence post, skewered.

His partner fired his weapon at someone Pacca couldn't see in the gloom. She scrambled to pull her damp clothes to order and get away from the line of fire.

The weapon in the militant's hand imploded, ripping through him, his blood mixing with the rain flowing into the plains.

A man—well, he appeared like a man at first— gracefully appeared out of the gloom and stood over her. He was covered in non-reflective dark goatskin leather from neck to boots that rippled around his muscles. His gloved hand held a glowing sword, which retracted into a staff as he extended his left hand towards her.

"Don't be afraid," his reassuring voice settled around her like a warm blanket.

For a moment, Pacca forgot about the death and devastation around her. Without understanding how or why she trusted him, she placed her hand in his and got zapped, like when she'd once touched an exposed live electrical wire in the house.

Her breath hitched just as his eyes widened. He must have felt the same sharp tingle.

He held her gaze as he tugged her up, his eyes the same golden glow as his weapon.

Now she could see him better.

He looked boyish rather than man, probably in his late teens. Only a few years older than her.

How could a person so young have such incredible power? He had defeated vicious opponents fiercely, like the superheroes she'd read in the comic books. Although, without the cape or body-clinging Lycra.

This boy-man's leather outfit was similar to the fictional Blade's, and his locs were packed in a ponytail with a leather band.

Pacca imagined his weapon to be the Sword of the Daywalker.

Except he was probably Masu Kare—warriors imbued with magical powers by the deities to protect the land. But those were fables, weren't they?

"Are you okay?" His voice was gentle as he guided her to the veranda, away from the rain.

"Y—yes. Thank you." She swallowed the lump in her throat. "How did you do that? Who are you? Are you Masu Kare?"

His lips tugged up at one corner as if he was amused by her questions. He didn't answer, though. Another man in a similar attire appeared at the edge of the house.

"I have to go. Will you be okay?" Concern wrinkled his brows.

Disappointment made her shoulders curl, and she wasn't sure why she felt an affinity to him. She didn't even know his name.

She lowered her head and shrugged. "I'll be fine."

She would have to be alright.

Live your best life—Mama's words.

Her mother was gone.

Tears built and spilt, running down her cheeks.

The young man wrapped his arms around her shoulders and held her without speaking. Nothing needed to be said. His actions were enough proof that he cared for her plight.

Comforted, she leaned back. "I'm alright, now. You should go and help other people."

He stepped aside and placed a gold coin in her hand. "If you ever need anything, present this seal, and you will be taken care of."

"Thank you. How can I become Masu Kare?"

She never wanted to feel as terrified and helpless as she felt today. She wanted to be able to protect herself and others if necessary. If she'd been Masu Kare, her mother would still be alive.

"That's for the gods to bestow if they deem you suitable. The first step is to take the coin to Bareki Academy and enrol into the warrior programme."

He smiled as he walked away. When he reached the corner, he said, "and my name is Prince Sefu Bahati."

Then he was gone.

OTHER BOOKS BY LOVE AFRICA PRESS

The Resolute Prince by Nana Prah
Love on a Mission by Jomi Oyel
Note Worthy by Dhasi Mwale
Fading Face by Jonah Igwe

CONNECT WITH US

Facebook.com/LoveAfricaPress
Twitter.com/LoveAfricaPress
Instagram.com/LoveAfricaPress

SIGN UP TO OUR NEWSLETTER
https://www.loveafricapress.com/newsletter